Ruskin Bond's first novel, *The Room on the Roof*, written when he was seventeen, received the John Llewellyn Rhys Memorial Prize in 1957. Since then he has written a number of novellas (including *Vagrants in the Valley*, *A Flight of Pigeons* and *Mr Oliver's Diary*) essays, poems and children's books, many of which have been published in Puffin Books. He has also written over 500 short stories and articles that have appeared in magazines and anthologies. He received the Sahitya Akademi Award in 1993, the Padma Shri in 1999 and the Padma Bhushan in 2014.

Ruskin Bond was born in Kasauli, Himachal Pradesh, and grew up in Jamnagar, Dehradun, New Delhi and Simla. As a young man, he spent four years in the Channel Islands and London. He returned to India in 1955. He now lives in Landour, Mussoorie, with his adopted family.

Also in Puffin by Ruskin Bond

RUSKIN BOND

BOND

RUSTY
The Boy from the Hills

ILLUSTRATIONS BY
ARCHANA SREENIVASAN

PUFFIN BOOKS

PUFFIN BOOKS

USA | Canada | UK | Ireland | Australia
New Zealand | India | South Africa | China

Puffin Books is part of the Penguin Random House group of companies
whose addresses can be found at global.penguinrandomhouse.com

Published by Penguin Random House India Pvt. Ltd
7th Floor, Infinity Tower C, DLF Cyber City,
Gurgaon 122 002, Haryana, India

First published in Puffin by Penguin Books India 2003
This illustrated edition published 2014

Copyright © Ruskin Bond 2003

All rights reserved

10 9 8 7 6 5 4 3 2

This is a work of fiction. Names, characters, places and incidents are either the
product of the author's imagination or are used fictitiously and any resemblance
to any actual person, living or dead, events or locales is entirely coincidental.

ISBN 9780143333432

Typeset in Adobe Garamond Pro by Ram Das Lal, New Delhi

Printed at Repro Knowledgecast Limited, Thane

www.penguin.co.in

Contents

Author's Note

STORIES FEATURING RUSTY (my alter ego) go back to my beginnings as a writer, when the sixteen-year-old Rusty appeared as the central character in *The Room on the Roof*, my first novel. Since then he has turned up in stories written at different periods of my life— sometimes as a small boy, sometimes as a schoolboy or teenager or young adult. These stories first appeared in magazines, then in diverse collections. They formed scattered episodes in the life of Rusty.

I have now brought them together in sequence, to create a certain continuity, presenting Rusty's experiences and adventures in the order in which they actually took place. In this volume, the stories describe Rusty as a small boy, and go up to the time of his father's death. The next volume will depict Rusty in his teens. In this way I hope to present the life of Rusty in as complete and interesting a manner as possible.

I would like to thank Udayan Mitra and Anjana Ramakrishnan for their expert editorial help in the presentation of this series of Rusty stories. I am also grateful to Shubhadarshini Singh for her sensitive portrayal of Rusty's story in her Hindi television serial *Ek Tha Rusty*, produced a few years ago.

Landour, Mussoorie   Ruskin Bond
October 2014

All Creatures
Great and Small

INSTEAD OF HAVING brothers and sisters to grow up with in India, I had as my companions an odd assortment of pets, which included a monkey, a tortoise, a python and a Great Indian Hornbill. The person responsible for all this wildlife in the home was my paternal grandfather. As the house was his own, other members of the family could not prevent him from keeping a large variety of pets, though they could certainly voice their objections; and as most of the household consisted of women—my grandmother and visiting aunts (my father was working for a firm dealing in rubber in Burma at the time and I hadn't seen my mother since her separation from Father when I was only four)—Grandfather and I had to be alert and resourceful in dealing with them. We saw eye to eye on the subject of pets, and whenever

Grandmother decided it was time to get rid of a tame white rat or a squirrel,

I would conceal them in a hole in the jackfruit tree; but unlike my aunts, she was generally tolerant of Grandfather's hobby, and even took a liking to some of our pets.

Grandfather's house and menagerie were in Dehra and I remember travelling there in a horse-drawn buggy. There were cars in those days but in the foothills a tonga was just as good, almost as fast, and certainly more dependable when it came to getting across the swift little Tons river.

During the rains, when the river flowed strong and deep, it was impossible to get across except on a hand-operated ropeway; but in the dry months, the horse went splashing through, the carriage wheels churning through clear mountain water. If the horse found the going difficult, we removed our shoes, rolled up our skirts or trousers, and waded across.

When Grandfather first went to stay in Dehra, the only way of getting there was by the night mail coach. Mail ponies, he told me, were difficult animals, always attempting to turn around and get into the coach with the passengers. It was only when the coachman used his whip liberally, and reviled the ponies' ancestors as far back as their third and fourth generations that the beasts could be persuaded to move. And once they started, there was no stopping them. It was a gallop all the way to the first stage, where the ponies were changed to the accompaniment of a bugle blown by the coachman.

At one stage of the journey drums were beaten; and if it was night, torches were lit to keep away the wild elephants who, resenting the approach of this clumsy caravan, would sometimes trumpet a challenge and throw the ponies into confusion.

Grandfather disliked dressing up and going out, and was only too glad to send everyone shopping or to the pictures—Harold Lloyd and Eddie Cantor were the favourites at Dehra's small cinema—so that he could be left alone to feed his pets and potter about in the garden. There were a lot of animals to be fed, including, for a time, a pair of Great Danes who had such enormous appetites that we were forced to give them away to a more affluent family.

The Great Danes were gentle creatures, and I would sit astride one of them and go for rides round the garden. In spite of their size, they were very sure-footed and never knocked over people or chairs. A little monkey, like Toto, did much more damage.

Grandfather bought Toto from a tonga-owner for the sum of five rupees. The tonga-man used to keep the little red monkey tied to a feeding trough, and Toto looked so out of place there—almost conscious of his own incongruity—that Grandfather immediately decided to add him to our menagerie.

Toto was really a cute little monkey. His bright eyes sparkled with mischief beneath deep-set eyebrows, and his teeth, a pearly white, were often on display in a smile that frightened the life out of elderly Anglo-Indian ladies. His hands were not those of a Tallulah Bankhead (Grandfather's only favourite actress), but were shrivelled and dried-up, as though they had been pickled in the sun for many years. But his fingers were quick and restless; and his tail, while adding to his good looks—Grandfather maintained that a tail would add to anyone's good looks—often performed the service of a third hand. He could use it to hang from a branch, and it was capable of scooping up any delicacy that might be out of reach of his hands.

Grandmother, anticipating an outcry from other relatives, always raised objections when Grandfather brought home some new bird or animal, and so for a while we managed to keep Toto's presence a secret by lodging him in a little closet opening into my bedroom wall. But in a few hours he managed to dispose of Grandmother's ornamental wallpaper and the better part of my school blazer. He was transferred to the stables for a day or two, and then Grandfather had to make a trip to neighbouring Saharanpur to collect his railway pension and, anxious to keep Toto out of trouble, he decided to take the monkey along with him.

Unfortunately, I could not accompany Grandfather on this trip, but he told me about it afterwards.

A black kitbag was provided for Toto. When the strings of the bag were tied, there was no means of escape from within, and the canvas was too strong for Toto to bite his way through. His initial efforts to get out only had the effect of making the bag roll about on the floor, or occasionally jump in the air—an exhibition that attracted a curious crowd of onlookers on the Dehra railway platform.

Toto remained in the bag as far as Saharanpur, but while Grandfather was producing his ticket at the railway turnstile, Toto managed to get his hands through the aperture where the bag was tied, loosened the strings, and suddenly thrust his head through the opening.

The poor ticket-collector was visibly alarmed, but with great presence of mind, and much to the annoyance of Grandfather, he said, 'Sir, you have a dog with you. You'll have to pay for it accordingly.'

'It's not a dog!' said Grandfather indignantly. 'This is a baby monkey of the species macacus—mischievous, closely related to the human species homus-horriblis! And there is no charge for babies!'

'It's as big as a cat,' said the ticket-collector.

'Next you'll be asking to see his mother,' snapped Grandfather.

In vain did Grandfather take Toto out of the bag to prove that a monkey was not a dog or even a quadruped. The ticket-collector, now thoroughly annoyed, insisted on classifying Toto as a dog; and three rupees and four annas had to be handed over as his fare. Then Grandfather, out of sheer spite, took out from his pocket a small live tortoise that he happened to have with him, and asked testily, 'What must I pay for this, since you charge for all creatures great and small?'

The ticket-collector retreated a pace or two, then advancing again with caution, he subjected the tortoise to a grave and knowledgeable stare.

'No ticket is necessary, sir,' he finally declared. 'There is no charge for insects.'

When we discovered that Toto's favourite pastime was catching mice, we were able to persuade Grandmother to let us keep him. The unsuspecting mice would emerge from their holes at night to pick up any corn left over by our pony; and to get at it they had to run the gauntlet of Toto's section of the stable. He knew this, and would pretend to be asleep, keeping, however, one eye open. A mouse would make a rush—in vain; Toto, as swift as a cat, would have his paws upon him . . . Grandmother decided to put his talents to constructive use by tying him up one night in the larder, where a guerrilla band of mice were playing havoc with our food supplies.

Toto was removed from his comfortable bed of straw in the stable, and chained up in the larder, beneath shelves of jam pots and other delicacies. The night was a long and miserable one for Toto, who must have wondered what he had done to deserve such treatment. The mice scampered about the place, while he, most uncatlike, lay curled up in a soup tureen, trying to snatch some sleep. At dawn, the mice returned to their holes; Toto awoke, scratched himself, emerged from the soup tureen, and looked about for something to eat. The jam pots attracted his notice, and it did not take him long to prise open the covers. Grandmother's treasured jams—she had made most of them herself— disappeared in an amazingly short time. I was present when she opened the door to see how many mice Toto had caught. Even the rain-god Indra could not have looked more terrible when planning a thunderstorm;

and the imprecations Grandmother hurled at Toto were surprising coming from someone who had been brought up in the genteel Victorian manner.

The monkey was later reinstated in Grandmother's favour. A great treat for him on cold winter evenings was the large bowl of warm water provided by Grandmother for his bath. He would bathe himself, first of all gingerly testing the temperature of the water with his fingers. Leisurely, he would step into the bath, first one foot, then the other, as he had seen me doing, until he was completely sitting down in it. Once comfortable, he would take the soap in his hands or feet, and rub himself all over. When he found the water becoming cold, he would get out and run as quickly as he could to the fire, where his coat soon dried. If anyone laughed at him during this performance, he would look extremely hurt, and refuse to go on with his ablutions.

One day Toto nearly succeeded in boiling himself to death.

The large kitchen kettle had been left on the fire to boil for tea; and Toto, finding himself for a few minutes alone with it, decided to take the lid off. On discovering that the water inside was warm, he got into the kettle with the intention of having a bath, and sat down with his head protruding from the opening. This was very pleasant for some time, until the water began to simmer. Toto raised himself a little, but finding it cold outside, sat down again. He continued standing and sitting for some time, not having the courage to face the cold air. Had it not been for the timely arrival of Grandmother, he would have been cooked alive.

If there is a part of the brain specially devoted to mischief, that part must have been largely developed in Toto. He was always tearing things to bits, and whenever one of my aunts came near him, he made every effort to get hold of her dress and tear a hole in it. A variety of aunts frequently came to stay with my grandparents, but during Toto's stay they limited their visits to a day or two, much to Grandfather's relief and Grandmother's annoyance.

Toto, however, took a liking to Grandmother, in spite of the beatings he often received from her. Whenever she allowed him the liberty, he would lie quietly in her lap instead of scrambling all over her as he did on most people.

Toto lived with us for over a year, but the following winter, after too much bathing, he caught pneumonia. Grandmother wrapped him in flannel, and Grandfather gave him a diet of chicken soup and Irish stew, but Toto did not recover. He was buried in the garden, under his favourite mango tree. Perhaps it was just as well that Toto was no longer with us when Grandfather

Toto did not recover. He was buried on the ... under his favourite mango tree. Perhaps it was well that Toto was no longer with us when Grandmother brought home the python, or his demise might have been less conventional. Small monkeys are a favourite delicacy with pythons.

Grandmother was tolerant of most birds and animals, but she drew the line at reptiles. She said they made her blood run cold. Even a handsome, sweet-tempered chameleon had to be given up. Grandfather should have known that there was little chance of his being allowed to keep the python. It was about four feet long, a young one, when Grandfather bought it from a snake charmer for six rupees, impressing the bazaar crowd by slinging it across his shoulders and walking home with it. Grandmother nearly fainted at the sight of the python curled round Grandfather's throat.

'You'll be strangled!' she cried. 'Get rid of it at once!'

'Nonsense,' said Grandfather. 'He's only a young fellow. He'll soon get used to us.'

'Will he, indeed?' said Grandmother. 'But I have no intention of getting used to him. You know quite well that my niece Mabel is coming to stay with us tomorrow. She'll leave us the minute she knows there's a snake in the house.'

'Well, perhaps we ought to show it to her as soon as she arrives,' said Grandfather, who did not look forward to fussy Aunt Mabel's visits any more than I did.

'You'll do no such thing,' said Grandmother.

'Well, I can't let it loose in the garden,' said Grandfather with an innocent expression. 'It might find its way into the poultry house, and then where would we be?'

'How exasperating you are!' grumbled Grandmother. 'Lock the creature in the bathroom, go back to the bazaar and find the man you bought it from, and get him to come and take it back.'

In my awestruck presence, Grandfather had to take the python into the bathroom, where he placed it in a steep-sided tin tub. Then he hurried off to the bazaar to look for the snake charmer, while Grandmother paced anxiously up and down the veranda. When he returned looking crestfallen, we knew he hadn't been able to find the man.

'You had better take it away yourself,' said Grandmother, in a relentless mood. 'Leave it in the jungle across the riverbed.'

'All right, but let me give it a feed first,' said Grandfather; and producing a plucked chicken, he took it into the bathroom, followed, in single file, by me, Grandmother, and a curious cook and gardener.

Grandfather threw open the door and stepped into the bathroom. I peeped round his legs, while the others remained well behind. We couldn't see the python anywhere.

'He's gone,' announced Grandfather. 'He must have felt hungry.'

'I hope he isn't too hungry,' I said.

'We left the window open,' said Grandfather, looking embarrassed.

A careful search was made of the house, the kitchen, the garden, the stable and the poultry shed, but the python couldn't be found anywhere.

'He'll be well away by now,' said Grandfather reassuringly.

'I certainly hope so,' said Grandmother, who was halfway between anxiety and relief.

Aunt Mabel arrived next day for a three-week visit, and for a couple of days Grandfather and I were a little apprehensive in case the python made a sudden reappearance; but on the third day, when he didn't show up, we felt confident that he had gone for good.

And then, towards evening, we were startled by a scream from the garden. Seconds later, Aunt Mabel came flying up the veranda steps, looking as though she had seen a ghost.

'In the guava tree!' she gasped. 'I was reaching for a guava, when I saw it staring at me. The *look* in its eyes! As though it would *devour* me—'

'Calm down, my dear,' urged Grandmother,

sprinkling her with eau de cologne. 'Calm down and tell us what you saw.'

'A snake!' sobbed Aunt Mabel. 'A great boa constrictor. It must have been twenty feet long! In the guava tree. Its eyes were terrible. It looked at me in such a *queer* way . . .'

My grandparents looked significantly at each other, and Grandfather said, 'I'll go out and kill it,' and sheepishly taking hold of an umbrella, sallied out into the garden. But when he reached the guava tree, the python had disappeared.

'Aunt Mabel must have frightened it away,' I said.

'Quiet, Rusty,' said Grandfather. 'We mustn't speak of your aunt in that way.' But his eyes were alive with laughter.

After this incident, the python began to make a series of appearances, often in the most unexpected places. Aunt Mabel had another fit of hysterics when she saw him admiring her from under a cushion. She packed her bags, and Grandmother made us intensify the hunt.

Next morning, I saw the python curled up on the dressing table, gazing at his reflection in the mirror. I went for Grandfather, but by the time we returned, the python had moved elsewhere. A little later he was seen in the garden again. Then he was back on the dressing table, admiring himself in the mirror. Evidently, he had become enamoured of his own reflection. Grandfather observed that perhaps the attention he was receiving from everyone had made him a little conceited.

'He's trying to look better for Aunt Mabel,' I said, a remark that I instantly regretted, because Grandmother overheard it, and brought the flat of her broad hand down on my head.

'Well, now we know his weakness,' said Grandfather.

'Are you trying to be funny too?' demanded Grandmother, looking her most threatening.

'I only meant he was becoming very vain,' said Grandfather hastily. 'It should be easier to catch him now.'

He set about preparing a large cage with a mirror at one end. In the cage he left a juicy chicken and various other delicacies, and fitted up the opening with a trapdoor. Aunt Mabel had already left by the time we had this trap ready, but we had to go on with the project because we couldn't have the python prowling about the house indefinitely.

For a few days nothing happened, and then, as I was leaving for school one morning, I saw the python curled up in the cage. He had eaten everything left out for him, and was relaxing in front of the mirror with something resembling a smile on his face—if you can imagine a python smiling . . . I lowered the trapdoor gently, but the python took no notice; he was in raptures over his handsome reflection. Grandfather and the gardener put the cage in the pony trap, and made a journey to the other side of the riverbed. They left the cage in the jungle, with the trapdoor open.

'He made no attempt to get out,' said Grandfather later. 'And I didn't have the heart to take the mirror away. It's the first time I've seen a snake fall in love.'

And the frogs have sung their old song in the mud . . . This was Grandfather's favourite quotation from Virgil, and he used it whenever we visited the rainwater pond behind the house where there were quantities of mud and frogs and the occasional water buffalo. Grandfather had once brought a number of frogs into the house. He had put them in a ceramic jar, left them on a windowsill, and then forgotten all about them. At about four o'clock in the morning the entire household was awakened by a loud and fearful noise, and Grandmother and several nervous relatives gathered in their nightclothes on the veranda. Their timidity changed to fury when they discovered that the ghastly sounds had come from Grandfather's frogs. Seeing the dawn breaking, the frogs had with one accord begun their morning song.

Grandmother wanted to throw the frogs, jar and all,

out of the window; but Grandfather said that if he gave the jar a good shaking, the frogs would remain quiet. He was obliged to keep awake, in order to shake the jar whenever the frogs showed any inclination to break into song. Fortunately for all concerned, the next day a servant took the top off the jar to see what was inside. The sight of several big frogs so startled him that he ran off without replacing the cover; the frogs jumped out and presumably found their way back to the pond.

It became a habit with me to visit the pond on my own, in order to explore its banks and shallows. Taking off my shoes, I would wade into the muddy water up to my knees to pluck the water lilies that floated on the surface.

One day I found the pond already occupied by several buffaloes. Their keeper, a boy a little older than me, was swimming about in the middle. Instead of climbing out on to the bank, he would pull himself up on the back of one of his buffaloes, stretch his naked brown body out on the animal's glistening wet hide, and start singing to himself.

When he saw me staring at him from across the pond, he smiled, showing gleaming white teeth in a dark, sun-burnished face. He invited me to join him in a swim. I told him I couldn't swim, and he offered to teach me. I hesitated, knowing that Grandmother held strict and old-fashioned views about mixing with village children; but, deciding that Grandfather—who sometimes smoked a hookah on the sly—would get me out of any trouble that might occur, I took the bold step of accepting the boy's offer. Once taken, the step did not seem so bold.

He dived off the back of his buffalo, and swam across to me. And I, having removed my clothes, followed his instructions until I was floundering about among the water lilies. His name was Ramu, and he promised to give me swimming lessons every afternoon; and so it was during the afternoons—specially summer afternoons when everyone was asleep—that we usually met. Before long I was able to swim across the pond to sit with Ramu astride a contented buffalo, the great beast standing like an island in the middle of a muddy ocean.

Sometimes we would try racing the buffaloes, Ramu and I sitting on different mounts. But they were lazy creatures, and would leave one comfortable spot only to look for another, or, if they were in no mood for games, would roll over on their backs, taking us with them into the mud and green slime of the pond. Emerging in shades of green and khaki, I would slip into the house through the bathroom and bathe under the tap before getting into my clothes.

One afternoon Ramu and I found a small tortoise in the mud, sitting over a hole in which it had laid several eggs. Ramu kept the eggs for his dinner, and I presented the tortoise to Grandfather. He had a weakness for tortoises, and was pleased with this addition to his menagerie, giving it a large tub of water all to itself, with an island of rocks in the middle. The tortoise, however, was always getting out of the tub and wandering about the house. As it seemed able to look after itself quite well, we did not interfere. If one of the dogs bothered it too much, it would draw its head and legs into its shell and defy all their attempts at rough play.

Ramu came from a family of bonded labourers, and had received no schooling. But he was well-versed in folklore, and knew a great deal about birds and animals.

'Many birds are sacred,' said Ramu, as we watched a blue jay swoop down from a peepul tree and carry off a grasshopper. He told me that both the blue jay and the god Shiva were called Nilkanth. Shiva had a blue throat, like the bird, because out of compassion for the human race he had swallowed a deadly poison which was intended to destroy the world. Keeping the poison in his throat, he did not let it go any further.

'Are squirrels sacred?' I asked, seeing one sprint down the trunk of the peepul tree.

'Oh yes, Lord Krishna loved squirrels,' said Ramu.

'He would take them in his arms and stroke them with his long fingers. That is why they have four dark lines down their backs from head to tail. Krishna was very dark, and the lines are the marks of his fingers.'

Both Ramu and Grandfather were of the opinion that we should be more gentle with birds and animals and should not kill so many of them.

'It is also important that we respect them,' said Grandfather. 'We must acknowledge their rights. Everywhere, birds and animals are finding it more difficult to survive, because we are trying to destroy both them and their forests. They have to keep moving as the trees disappear.'

This was specially true of the forests near Dehra, where the tiger and the pheasant and the spotted deer were beginning to disappear.

Ramu and I spent many long summer afternoons at the pond. I still remember him with affection, though we never saw each other again after I left Dehra. He could not read or write, so we were unable to keep in touch. And neither his people, nor mine, knew of our friendship. The buffaloes and frogs had been our only confidants. They had accepted us as part of their own world, their muddy but comfortable pond. And when I left Dehra, both they and Ramu must have assumed that I would return again like the birds.

The Tree Lover

I WAS NEVER able to get over the feeling that plants and trees loved Grandfather with as much tenderness as he loved them. I was sitting beside him on the veranda steps one morning, when I noticed the tendril of a creeping vine that was trailing near my feet. As we sat there, in the soft sunshine of a north Indian winter, I saw that the tendril was moving very slowly away from me and towards Grandfather. Twenty minutes later it had crossed the veranda step and was touching Grandfather's feet.

There is probably a scientific explanation for the plant's behaviour—something to do with light and warmth—but I like to think that it moved that way simply because it was fond of Grandfather. One felt like drawing close to him. Sometimes when I sat alone beneath a tree I would feel a little lonely or lost; but as soon as Grandfather joined me, the garden would become a happy place, the tree itself more friendly.

Grandfather had served many years in the Indian Forest Service, and so it was natural that he should know and understand and like trees. On his retirement from the Service, he had built a bungalow on the outskirts of Dehra, planting trees all round it: limes, mangoes, oranges and guavas; also eucalyptus, jacaranda and the Persian lilac. In the fertile Doon valley, plants and trees grew tall and strong.

There were other trees in the compound before the house was built, including an old peepul which had forced its way through the walls of an abandoned outhouse, knocking the bricks down with its vigorous growth. Peepul trees are great show-offs. Even when there is no breeze, their broad-chested, slim-waisted leaves will spin like tops, determined to attract your attention and invite you into the shade.

Grandmother had wanted the peepul tree cut down, but Grandfather had said, 'Let it be. We can always build another outhouse.'

Our gardener, Govind, who was a Hindu, was pleased that we had allowed the tree to live. Peepul trees are sacred to Hindus, and some people believe that ghosts live in the branches of these trees.

'If we cut the tree down, wouldn't the ghosts go away?' I asked.

'I don't know,' said Grandfather. 'Perhaps they'd come into the house.'

Govind wouldn't walk under the tree at night. He said that once, when he was a youth, he had wandered beneath a peepul tree late at night, and that something heavy had fallen with a thud on his shoulders. Since then he had always walked with a slight stoop, he explained.

'Nonsense,' said Grandmother, who didn't believe in ghosts. 'He got his stoop from squatting on his haunches year after year, weeding with that tiny spade of his!'

I never saw any ghosts in our peepul tree. There are peepul trees all over India, and people sometimes leave offerings of milk and flowers beneath them to keep the spirits happy. But since no one left any offerings under our tree, I expect the ghosts left in disgust, to look for peepul trees where there was both board and lodging.

Grandfather was about sixty, a lean active man who still rode his bicycle at great speed. He had stopped climbing trees a year previously, when he had got to the top of the jackfruit tree and had been unable to come down again. We had to fetch a ladder for him.

Grandfather bathed quite often but got back into

his gardening clothes immediately after the bath. During meals, ladybirds or caterpillars would sometimes walk off his shirtsleeves and wander about on the tablecloth, and this always annoyed Grandmother.

She grumbled at Grandfather a lot, but he didn't mind, because he knew she loved him.

My favourite tree was the banyan which grew behind the house. Its spreading branches, which hung to the ground and took root again, formed a number of twisting passageways. The tree was older than the house, older than my grandparents; I could hide in its branches, behind a screen of thick green leaves, and spy on the world below.

The banyan tree was a world in itself, populated with small animals and large insects. While the leaves were still pink and tender, they would be visited by the delicate map butterfly, who left her eggs in their care. The 'honey' on the leaves—a sweet, sticky smear—also attracted the little striped squirrels, who soon grew used to having me in the tree and became quite bold, accepting gram from my hand.

At night the tree was visited by the hawk cuckoo. Its shrill nagging cry kept us awake on hot summer nights. Indians called the bird 'Paos-ala', which means

'Rain is coming!' But according to Grandfather, when the bird was in full cry, it seemed to be shouting, 'Oh dear, oh dear! How very hot it's getting! We feel it . . . we feel it . . . WE FEEL IT!'

Grandfather wasn't content with planting trees in our garden. During the rains we would walk into the jungle beyond the riverbed, armed with cuttings and saplings, and these we would plant in the forest, beside the tall sal and shisham trees.

'But no one ever comes here,' I protested, the first time we did this. 'Who is going to see them?'

'We're not planting for people only,' said Grandfather. 'We're planting for the forest—and for the birds and animals who live here and need more food and shelter.'

He told me how men, and not only birds and animals, needed trees—for keeping the desert away, for attracting rain, for preventing the banks of rivers from being washed away and for wild plants and grasses to grow beneath.

'And for timber?' I asked, pointing to the sal and shisham trees.

'Yes, Rusty, and for timber. But men are cutting down the trees without replacing them. For every tree that's felled, we must plant *two*. Otherwise, one day there'll be no forests at all, and the world will become one great desert.'

The thought of a world without trees became a sort of nightmare for me—it's one reason why I shall never want to live on the treeless moon—and I helped Grandfather in his tree planting with even greater enthusiasm. He taught me a poem by George Morris, and we would recite it together:

Woodman, spare that tree!

Touch not a single bough!

In youth it sheltered me,

And I'll protect it now.

'One day the trees will move again,' said Grandfather. 'They've been standing still for thousands of years, but one day they'll move again. There was a time when trees could walk about like people, but along came the Devil and cast a spell over them, rooting them to one place. But they're always trying to move—see how they reach out with their arms! And some of them, like the banyan tree with its travelling roots, manage to get quite far!'

In the autumn, Grandfather took me to the hills. The deodars (Indian cedars), oaks, chestnuts and maples were very different from the trees I had seen in Dehra. The broad leaves of the horse chestnut had turned yellow, and smooth brown chestnuts lay scattered on the roads. Grandfather and I filled our pockets with them, then climbed the slope of a bare hill and started planting the chestnuts in the ground.

I don't know if they ever came up, because I never went there again. Goats and cattle grazed freely on the hill, and, if the trees did come up in the spring, they may well have been eaten; but I like to think that somewhere in the foothills of the Himalayas there is a grove of chestnut trees, and that birds and flying foxes and cicadas have made their homes in them.

Back in Dehra, we found an island, a small rocky island in the middle of a dry riverbed. It was one of those riverbeds, so common in the Doon valley, which are completely dry in summer but flooded during the monsoon rains. A small mango tree was growing in the middle of the island, and Grandfather said, 'If a mango can grow here, so can other trees.'

As soon as the rains set in—and while the river could still be crossed—we set out with a number of tamarind, laburnum and coral tree saplings and cuttings, and spent the day planting them on the island.

When the monsoon set in, the trees appeared to be flourishing.

The monsoon season was the time for rambling about. At every turn there was something new to see. Out of earth and rock and leafless bough, the magic touch of the monsoon rains had brought life and greenness.

You could almost see the broad-leaved vines grow. Plants sprang up in the most unlikely places. A peepul would take root in the ceiling, a mango would sprout on the windowsill. We did not like to remove them; but they had to go, if the house was to be kept from falling down.

'If you want to live in a tree, it's all right by me,' said Grandmother. 'But I like having a roof over my head, and I'm not going to have it brought down by the jungle!'

The common monsoon sights along the Indian roads were always picturesque—the wide plains, with great herds of smoke-coloured, delicate-limbed cattle being driven slowly home for the night, accompanied by several ungainly buffaloes, and flocks of goats and black long-tailed sheep. Then you came to a pond, where some buffaloes were enjoying themselves, with no part of them visible but the tips of their noses, while on their backs were a number of merry children, perfectly and happily naked.

The banyan tree really came to life during the monsoon, when the branches were thick with scarlet figs. Humans couldn't eat the berries, but the many birds that gathered in the tree—gossipy rosy pastors, quarrelsome mynahs, cheerful bulbuls and coppersmiths, and sometimes a noisy, bullying crow—

feasted on them. And when night fell and the birds were resting, the dark flying foxes flapped heavily about the tree, chewing and munching loudly as they clambered over the branches.

The tree crickets were a band of willing artists who started their singing at almost any time of the day but preferably in the evenings. Delicate, pale-green creatures with transparent wings, they were hard to find amongst the lush monsoon foliage, but once found, a tap on the bush or leaf on which one of them sat would put an immediate end to its performance.

At the height of the monsoon, the banyan tree was like an orchestra with the musicians constantly tuning up. Birds, insects and squirrels welcomed the end of the hot weather and the cool quenching relief of the monsoon.

A toy flute in my hands, I would try adding my shrill piping to theirs. But they must have thought poorly of my piping, for, whenever I played, the birds and the insects kept a pained and puzzled silence.

I wonder if they missed me when I went away—for two years later, when I was nine, I went to join my father in Java. Later, after I returned to India with him, I was sent to a boarding school in Simla. Because Dehra wasn't all that far from Simla, I was able to visit my grandmother off and on whenever the school closed for holidays. Grandmother lived all by herself by that time as Grandfather had passed away all of a sudden. In the garden, on my first visit to Dehra from school, I found that the banyan tree had grown over the wall and along part of the pavement, almost as though it had tried to follow Grandfather. I walked out of town towards the riverbed.

It was February, and as I looked across the dry water course, my eye was caught by the spectacular red plumes of the coral blossom. In contrast to the dry riverbed, the island was a small green paradise. When I walked across to the trees, I noticed that a number of squirrels had come to live in them. And a koel (a sort of crow-pheasant) challenged me with a mellow 'who-are-you, who-are-you . . .'

But the trees seemed to know me. They whispered among themselves and beckoned me nearer. And looking around, I noticed that other small trees and wild plants and grasses had sprung up under the protection of the trees we had placed there.

The trees had multiplied! They were moving. In one small corner of the world, Grandfather's dream was coming true, and the trees were moving again.

A Tiger in the House

TIMOTHY, THE TIGER cub, was discovered by Grandfather on a hunting expedition in the Terai jungle near Dehra.

Grandfather was no shikari, but as he knew the forests of the Siwalik hills better than most people, he was persuaded to accompany the party—it consisted of several Very Important Persons from Delhi—to advise on the terrain and the direction the beaters should take once a tiger had been spotted.

The camp itself was sumptuous—seven large tents (one for each shikari), a dining tent, and a number of servants' tents. The dinner was very good, as Grandfather admitted afterwards; it was not often that one saw hot-water plates, finger-glasses, and seven or eight courses in a tent in the jungle! But that was how things were done in the days of the Viceroys . . . There were also some fifteen elephants, four of them with howdahs for the shikaris, and the others specially trained for taking part in the beat.

The sportsmen never saw a tiger, nor did they shoot anything else, though they saw a number of deer, peacock and wild boar. They were giving up all hope of finding a tiger, and were beginning to shoot at jackals, when Grandfather, strolling down the forest path at some distance from the rest of the party, discovered a little tiger about eighteen inches long, hiding among the intricate roots of a banyan tree. Grandfather picked him up, and brought him home after the camp had broken up. He had the distinction of being the only member of the party to have bagged any game, dead or alive.

At first the tiger cub, who was named Timothy by Grandmother, was brought up entirely on milk given to him in a feeding bottle by our cook, Mahmoud. But the milk proved too rich for him, and he was put on a diet of raw mutton and cod liver oil, to be followed later by a more tempting diet of pigeons and rabbits.

Timothy was provided with two companions—Toto the monkey, who was bold enough to pull the young tiger by the tail, and then climb up the curtains if Timothy lost his temper, and a small mongrel puppy, found on the road by Grandfather.

At first Timothy appeared to be quite afraid of the

puppy, and darted back with a spring if it came too near. He would make absurd dashes at it with his large forepaws, and then retreat to a ridiculously safe distance.

Finally, he allowed the puppy to crawl on his back and rest there!

One of Timothy's favourite amusements was to stalk anyone who would play with him, and so, when I came to live with Grandfather, I became one of the tiger's favourites. With a crafty look in his glittering eyes, and his body crouching, he would creep closer and closer to me, suddenly making a dash for my feet, rolling over on his back and kicking with delight, and pretending to bite my ankles.

He was by this time the size of a full-grown retriever, and when I took him out for walks, people on the road would give us a wide berth. When he pulled hard on his chain, I had difficulty in keeping up with him. His favourite place in the house was the drawing room, and he would make himself comfortable on the long sofa, reclining there with great dignity, and snarling at anybody who tried to get him off.

Timothy had clean habits, and would scrub his face with his paws exactly like a cat. He slept at night in the cook's quarters, and was always delighted at being let out by him in the morning.

'One of these days,' declared Grandmother in her

prophetic manner, 'we are going to find Timothy sitting on Mahmoud's bed, and no sign of the cook except his clothes and shoes!'

Of course, it never came to that, but when Timothy was about six months old a change came over him; he grew steadily less friendly. When out for a walk with me, he would try to steal away to stalk a cat or someone's pet Pekinese. Sometimes at night we would hear frenzied cackling from the poultry house, and in the morning there would be feathers lying all over the veranda. Timothy had to be chained up more often. And, finally, when he began to stalk Mahmoud about the house with what looked like villainous intent, Grandfather decided it was time to transfer him to a zoo.

The nearest zoo was at Lucknow, two hundred miles away. Reserving a first-class compartment for himself and Timothy—no one would share a compartment with them—Grandfather took him to Lucknow where the zoo authorities were only too glad to receive as a gift a well-fed and fairly civilized tiger.

About six months later, when my grandparents were visiting relatives in Lucknow, Grandfather took the opportunity of calling at the zoo to see how Timothy was getting on. I was not there to accompany him, but I heard all about it when he returned to Dehra.

Arriving at the zoo, Grandfather made straight for the particular cage in which Timothy had been interned. The tiger was there, crouched in a corner, full-grown and with a magnificent striped coat.

'Hello, Timothy!' said Grandfather and, climbing the railing with ease, he put his arm through the bars of the cage.

The tiger approached the bars, and allowed Grandfather to put both hands around his head. Grandfather stroked the tiger's forehead and tickled his ear, and, whenever he growled, smacked him across the mouth, which was his old way of keeping him quiet.

He licked Grandfather's hands and only sprang away when a leopard in the next cage snarled at him. Grandfather 'shooed' the leopard away, and the tiger returned to lick his hands; but every now and then the leopard would rush at the bars, and the tiger would slink back to his corner.

A number of people had gathered to watch the reunion when a keeper pushed his way through the crowd and asked Grandfather what he was doing.

'I'm talking to Timothy,' said Grandfather. 'Weren't you here when I gave him to the zoo six months ago?'

'I haven't been here very long,' said the surprised keeper. 'Please continue your conversation. But I have never been able to touch him myself, he is always very bad-tempered.'

'Why don't you put him somewhere else?' suggested Grandfather. 'That leopard keeps frightening him. I'll go and see the Superintendent about it.'

Grandfather went in search of the Superintendent of the zoo, but found that he had gone home early; and so, after wandering about the zoo for a little while, he returned to Timothy's cage to say goodbye. It was beginning to get dark.

He had been stroking and slapping Timothy for about five minutes when he found another keeper observing him with some alarm. Grandfather recognized him as the keeper who had been there when Timothy had first come to the zoo.

'*You* remember me,' said Grandfather. 'Now why don't you transfer Timothy to another cage, away from this stupid leopard?'

'But—sir—' stammered the keeper, 'it is not your tiger.'

'I know, I know,' said Grandfather testily. 'I realize he is no longer mine. But you might at least take a suggestion or two from me.'

'I remember your tiger very well,' said the keeper. 'He died two months ago.'

'Died!' exclaimed Grandfather.

'Yes, sir, of pneumonia. This tiger was trapped in the hills only last month, and he is very dangerous!'

Grandfather could think of nothing to say. The tiger was still licking his arm, with increasing relish. Grandfather took what seemed to him an age to withdraw his hand from the cage.

With his face near the tiger's he mumbled, 'Goodnight, Timothy,' and giving the keeper a scornful look, walked briskly out of the zoo.

Monkey Trouble

SOON AFTER TOTO passed away, Grandfather bought another monkey—Tutu—from a street entertainer for the sum of ten rupees. The man had three monkeys. Tutu was the smallest but the most mischievous. She was tied up most of the time. The little monkey looked so miserable with a collar and chain that Grandfather decided it would be much happier in our home. His weakness for keeping unusual pets was something that I, at the age of seven, used to heartily encourage.

Grandmother at first objected to having another monkey in the house since she had been especially fond of Toto and believed that Toto could never be replaced in her affections. 'You have enough pets as it is,' she said, referring to Grandfather's goat, several white mice, and a small tortoise.

'But I don't have any,' I said.

39

'You're wicked enough for two monkeys. One boy in the house is all I can take.'

'Ah, but Tutu isn't a boy,' said Grandfather triumphantly. 'This is a little girl monkey!'

Grandmother gave in. She had always wanted a little girl in the house. She believed girls were less troublesome than boys. Tutu was to prove her wrong.

She was a pretty little monkey. One of the first things I taught her was to shake hands, and this she insisted on doing with all who visited the house. Peppery Major Malik would have to stoop and shake hands with Tutu before he could enter the drawing room, otherwise she would climb on his shoulder and stay there, roughing up his hair and playing with his moustache.

My uncle Ken, Granny's nephew who came to stay with us now and then, couldn't stand any of our pets and took a particular dislike to Tutu, who was always making faces at him. But as Uncle Ken was never in a job for long and depended on Grandfather's good-natured generosity, he had to shake hands with Tutu like everyone else.

Aunt Ruby, who had been staying with us for a few days, had not been informed of Tutu's arrival. Loud shrieks from her bedroom brought us running to see what was wrong. It was only Tutu trying on Aunt Ruby's petticoats! They were much too large, of course, and when Aunt Ruby entered the room all she saw was a faceless white blob jumping up and down on the bed.

We disentangled Tutu and soothed Aunt Ruby. I gave Tutu a bunch of sweet peas to make her happy. Granny didn't like anyone plucking her sweet peas, so I took some from Major Malik's garden while he was having his afternoon siesta.

Then Uncle Ken complained that his hairbrush was missing. We found Tutu sunning herself on the back veranda, using the hairbrush to scratch her armpits. I took it from her and handed it back to Uncle Ken with an apology, but he flung the brush away with an oath.

'Such a fuss about nothing,' I said. 'Tutu doesn't have fleas!'

'No, and she bathes more often than Ken,' said Grandfather, who had borrowed Aunt Ruby's shampoo for giving Tutu a bath.

All the same, Grandmother objected to Tutu being given the run of the house. Tutu had to spend her nights in the outhouse, in the company of the goat. They got on quite well, and it was not long before Tutu was seen sitting comfortably on the back of the goat, while the goat roamed the back garden in search of its favourite grass.

Aunt Ruby was a frequent taker of baths. This met with Tutu's approval—so much so, that one day, when Aunt Ruby had finished shampooing her hair she looked up through a lather of bubbles and soap suds to see Tutu sitting opposite her in the bath, following her example.

One day Aunt Ruby took us all by surprise. She announced that she had become engaged. We had always thought Aunt Ruby would never marry—she had often said so herself—but it appeared that the right man had now come along in the person of Rocky Fernandes, a schoolteacher from Goa.

Rocky was a tall, firm-jawed, good-natured man, a couple of years younger than Aunt Ruby. He had a fine baritone voice and sang in the manner of the great Nelson Eddy. As Grandmother liked baritone singers, Rocky was soon in her good books.

'But what on earth does he see in her?' Uncle Ken wanted to know.

'More than any girl has seen in you!' snapped Grandmother. 'Ruby's a fine girl. And they're both teachers. Maybe they can start a school of their own.'

Rocky visited the house quite often and brought me chocolates and cashewnuts, of which he seemed to have an unlimited supply. He also taught me several marching songs. Naturally I approved of Rocky. Aunt Ruby won my grudging admiration for having made such a wise choice.

One day I overheard them talking of going to the bazaar to buy an engagement ring. I decided I would go along too. But as Aunt Ruby had made it clear that she did not want me around I decided that I had better follow at a discreet distance. Tutu, becoming aware that a mission of some importance was underway, decided to follow me. But as I had not invited her along, she too decided to keep out of sight.

Once in the crowded bazaar, I was able to get quite close to Aunt Ruby and Rocky without being spotted. I waited until they had settled down in a large jewellery shop before sauntering past and spotting them as though by accident. Aunt Ruby wasn't too pleased at seeing me, but Rocky waved and called out, 'Come and join us! Help your aunt choose a beautiful ring!'

The whole thing seemed to be a waste of good money, but I did not say so—Aunt Ruby was giving me one of her more unloving looks.

'Look, these are pretty!' I said, pointing to some cheap, bright agates set in white metal. But Aunt Ruby wasn't looking. She was immersed in a case of diamonds.

'Why not a ruby for Aunt Ruby?' I suggested, trying to please her.

'That's her lucky stone,' said Rocky. 'Diamonds are the thing for engagement.' And he started singing a song about diamonds being a girl's best friend.

While the jeweller and Aunt Ruby were sifting through the diamond rings, and Rocky was trying out another tune, Tutu had slipped into the shop without being noticed by anyone but me. A little squeal of delight was the first sign she gave of her presence. Everyone looked up to see her trying on a pretty necklace.

'And what are those stones?' I asked.

'They look like pearls,' said Rocky.

'They *are* pearls,' said the shopkeeper, making a grab for them.

'It's that dreadful monkey!' cried Aunt Ruby. 'I knew that boy would bring her here!'

The necklace was already adorning Tutu's neck. I thought she looked rather nice in pearls, but she gave us no time to admire the effect. Springing out of our reach Tutu dodged around Rocky, slipped between my legs, and made for the crowded road. I ran after her, shouting to her to stop, but she wasn't listening.

There were no branches to assist Tutu in her progress, but she used the heads and shoulders of people as springboards and so made rapid headway through the bazaar.

The jeweller left his shop and ran after us. So did Rocky. So did several bystanders who had seen the incident. And others, who had no idea what it was all about, joined in the chase. As Grandfather used to say, 'In a crowd, everyone plays follow-the-leader even when they don't know who's leading.'

She tried to make her escape speedier by leaping on to the back of a passing scooterist. The scooter swerved into a fruit stall and came to a standstill under a heap of bananas, while the scooterist found himself in the arms of an indignant fruitseller. Tutu peeled a banana and ate part of it before deciding to move on.

From an awning she made an emergency landing on a washerman's donkey. The donkey promptly panicked and rushed down the road, while bundles of washing fell by the wayside. The washerman joined in the chase. Children on their way to school decided that there was something better to do than attend classes. With shouts of glee, they soon overtook their panting elders.

Tutu finally left the bazaar and took a road leading in the direction of our house. But knowing that she would be caught and locked up once she got home, she decided to end the chase by ridding herself of the necklace. Deftly removing it from her neck, she flung it in the small canal that ran down that road.

The jeweller, with a cry of anguish, plunged into the canal. So did Rocky. So did I. So did several other people, both adults and children. It was to be a treasure hunt!

Some twenty minutes later, Rocky shouted, 'I've found it!' Covered in mud, water lilies, ferns and tadpoles, we emerged from the canal, and Rocky presented the necklace to the relieved shopkeeper.

Everyone trudged back to the bazaar to find Aunt Ruby waiting in the shop, still trying to make up her mind about a suitable engagement ring.

Finally the ring was bought, the engagement was announced, and a date was set for the wedding.

'I don't want that monkey anywhere near us on our wedding day,' declared Aunt Ruby.

'We'll lock her up in the outhouse,' promised Grandfather. 'And we'll let her out only after you've left for your honeymoon.'

A few days before the wedding I found Tutu in the kitchen helping Grandmother prepare the wedding cake. Tutu often helped with the cooking, and, when Grandmother wasn't looking, added herbs, spices and other interesting items to the pots—so that occasionally we found a chilli in the custard or an onion in the jelly or a strawberry floating on the chicken soup.

Sometimes these additions improved a dish, sometimes they did not. Uncle Ken lost a tooth when he bit firmly into a sandwich which contained walnut shells.

I'm not sure exactly what went into that wedding

cake when Grandmother wasn't looking—she insisted that Tutu was always very well-behaved in the kitchen—but I did spot Tutu stirring in some red chilli sauce, bitter gourd seeds and a generous helping of eggshells!

It's true that some of the guests were not seen for several days after the wedding but no one said anything against the cake. Most people thought it had an interesting flavour.

The great day dawned, and the wedding guests made their way to the little church that stood on the outskirts of Dehra—a town with a church, two mosques and several temples.

I had offered to dress Tutu up as a bridesmaid and bring her along, but no one except Grandfather thought it was a good idea. So I decided to be an obedient boy and locked Tutu in the outhouse. I did, however, leave the skylight open a little. Grandmother had always said that fresh air was good for growing children, and I thought Tutu should have her share of it.

The wedding ceremony went without a hitch. Aunt Ruby looked a picture, and Rocky looked like a film star.

Grandfather played the organ, and did so with such gusto that the small choir could hardly be heard. Grandmother cried a little. I sat quietly in a corner, with the little tortoise on my lap.

When the service was over, we trooped out into the sunshine and made our way back to the house for the reception.

The feast had been laid out on tables in the garden. As the gardener had been left in charge, everything was in order. Tutu was on her best behaviour. She had, it appeared, used the skylight to avail of more fresh air outside, and now sat beside the three-tier wedding cake, guarding it against crows, squirrels and the goat. She greeted the guests with squeals of delight.

It was too much for Aunt Ruby. She flew at Tutu in a rage. And Tutu, sensing that she was not welcome, leapt away, taking with her the top tier of the wedding cake.

Led by Major Malik, we followed her into the orchard, only to find that she had climbed to the top of the jackfruit tree. From there she proceeded to pelt us with bits of wedding cake. She had also managed to get hold of a bag of confetti, and when she ran out of cake she showered us with confetti.

'That's more like it!' said the good-humoured Rocky. 'Now let's return to the party, folks!'

Uncle Ken remained with Major Malik, determined to chase Tutu away. He kept throwing stones into the tree, until he received a large piece of cake bang on his nose. Muttering threats, he returned to the party, leaving the Major to battle it out.

When the festivities were finally over, Uncle Ken took the unnecessary old car out of the garage and drove up to the veranda steps. He was going to drive Aunt Ruby and Rocky to the nearby hill resort of Mussoorie, where they would have their honeymoon.

Watched by family and friends, Aunt Ruby and Rocky climbed into the back seat. Aunt Ruby waved regally to everyone. She leant out of the window and offered me her cheek and I had to kiss her farewell. Everyone wished them luck.

As Rocky burst into song Uncle Ken opened the throttle and stepped on the accelerator. The car shot forward in a cloud of dust.

Rocky and Aunt Ruby continued to wave to us. And so did Tutu from her perch on the rear bumper! She was clutching a bag in her hands and showering confetti on all who stood in the driveway.

'They don't know Tutu's with them!' I exclaimed. 'She'll go all the way to Mussoorie! Will Aunt Ruby let her stay with them?'

'Tutu might ruin the honeymoon,' said Grandfather. 'But don't worry—our Ken will bring her back!'

Animals on the Track

'ALL ABOARD!' SHRIEKED Popeye, Grandmother's pet parrot, as the family climbed aboard the Lucknow Express. We were travelling from Dehra to Lucknow—Aunt Emily had invited us to spend a few days with her there—and as Grandmother had insisted on taking her parrot along, Grandfather and I had insisted on bringing along our pets as well. Grandfather had decided to have Timothy, his tiger, for company (this was before Timothy was given away to the zoo in Lucknow) and I had taken my small squirrel with me. We had thought it prudent to leave the python behind. Grandfather had only recently acquired this python—he had been quite sorry to get rid of the python he had earlier all because of Aunt Mabel's hysterics.

In those days the trains in India were not so crowded and it was possible to travel with a variety of creatures. Grandfather had decided to do things in style by travelling first-class, so we had a four-berth compartment of our own, and Timothy had an entire berth to himself. Later, everyone agreed that Timothy had behaved perfectly throughout the journey. Even the guard admitted that he could not have asked for a better passenger: no stealing from vendors, no shouting at coolies, no breaking of railway property, no spitting on the platform.

All the same, the journey was not without incident. Before we reached Lucknow, there was enough excitement for everyone.

To begin with, Popeye objected to vendors and other people poking their hands in at the windows. Before the train had pulled out of the Dehra station, he had nipped two fingers and tweaked a ticket-inspector's ear.

No sooner had the train started moving than Chips, my squirrel, emerged from my pocket to examine his surroundings. Before I could stop him, he was out of the compartment door, scurrying along the corridor.

Chips discovered that the train was a squirrel's paradise, almost all the passengers having bought large quantities of roasted peanuts before the train pulled out. He had no difficulty in making friends with both children and grown-ups, and it was an hour before he returned to our compartment, his tummy almost bursting.

'I think I'll go to sleep,' said Grandmother, covering herself with a blanket and stretching out on the berth opposite Timothy's. 'It's been a tiring day.'

'Aren't you going to eat anything?' asked Grandfather.

'I'm not hungry—I had some soup before we left. You two help yourselves from the tiffin-basket.'

Grandmother dozed off, and even Popeye started nodding, lulled to sleep by the clackety-clack of the wheels and the steady puffing of the steam engine.

'Well, I'm hungry,' I said. 'What did Granny make for us?'

'Ham sandwiches, boiled eggs, a roast chicken, gooseberry pie. It's all in the tiffin-basket under your berth.'

I tugged at the large basket and dragged it into the centre of the compartment. The straps were loosely tied. No sooner had I undone them than the lid flew open, and I let out a gasp of surprise.

In the basket was Grandfather's pet python, curled up contentedly on the remains of our dinner. Grandmother had insisted that we leave the python behind, and Grandfather had let it loose in the garden. Somehow, it had managed to snuggle itself into the tiffin-basket.

'Well, what are you staring at?' asked Grandfather from his corner.

'It's the python,' I said. 'And it's finished all our dinner.'

Grandfather joined me, and together we looked down at what remained of the food. Pythons don't chew, they swallow: outlined along the length of the large snake's sleek body were the distinctive shapes of a chicken, a pie, and six boiled eggs. We couldn't make out the ham sandwiches, but presumably these had been eaten too because there was no sign of them in the basket. Only a few apples remained. Evidently, the python did not care for apples.

Grandfather snapped the basket shut and pushed it back beneath the berth.

'We mustn't let Grandmother see him,' he said. 'She might think we brought him along on purpose.'

'Well, I'm hungry,' I complained. Just then Chips returned from one of his forays and presented me with a peanut.

'Thanks,' I said. 'If you keep bringing me peanuts all night, I might last until morning.'

But it was not long before I felt sleepy. Grandfather had begun to nod off and the only one who was wide awake was the squirrel, still intent on investigating distant compartments.

A little after midnight there was a great clamour at the end of the corridor. Grandfather and I woke up. Timothy growled in his sleep, and Popeye made complaining noises.

Suddenly there were cries of 'Saanp, saanp!' (Snake, snake!) Grandfather was on his feet in a moment. He looked under the berth. The tiffin-basket was empty.

'The python's out,' he said, and dashed out of our compartment in his pyjamas. I followed close behind.

About a dozen passengers were bunched together outside the washroom door.

'Anything wrong?' asked Grandfather casually.

'We can't get into the toilet,' said someone. 'There's a huge snake inside.'

'Let me take a look,' said Grandfather. 'I know all about snakes.'

The passengers made way for him, and he entered the washroom to find the python curled up in the washbasin. After its heavy meal it had become thirsty and, finding the lid of the tiffin-basket easy to prise up, had set out in search of water.

Grandfather gathered up the sleepy, overfed python and stepped out of the washroom. The passengers hastily made way for them.

'Nothing to worry about,' said Grandfather cheerfully. 'It's just a harmless young python. He's had his dinner already, so no one is in any danger!' And he marched back to our compartment with the python in his arms. As soon as I was inside, he bolted the door.

Grandmother was sitting up on her berth.

'I knew you'd do something foolish behind my back,' she scolded. 'You told me you'd left that creature behind, and all the time you've been hiding it from me.'

Grandfather tried to explain that we had nothing to do with it, that the python had snuggled itself into the tiffin-basket, but Grandmother was unconvinced. She declared that Grandfather couldn't live without the creature and that he had deliberately brought it along.

'What will Emily do when she sees it!' cried Grandmother despairingly.

My Aunt Emily was a schoolteacher in Lucknow and she was terrified of all reptiles, particularly snakes.

'We won't let her see it,' said Grandfather. 'Back it goes into the tiffin-basket.'

Early next morning the train steamed into Lucknow. Aunt Emily was on the platform to receive us.

Grandfather let all the other passengers get off before he emerged from the compartment with Timothy on a chain. I had Chips in my pocket, and a suitcase in each hand. Popeye stayed perched on Grandmother's shoulder, eyeing the busy platform with considerable distrust.

Aunt Emily, a lover of good food, immediately spotted the tiffin-basket, picked it up and said, 'It's not very heavy. I'll carry it out to the taxi. I hope you've kept something for me.'

'A whole chicken,' I said.

'We hardly ate anything,' said Grandfather.

'It's all yours, Aunty!' I added.

'Oh, good!' exclaimed Aunt Emily. 'It's been ages since I tasted something cooked by your grandmother.' And after that there was no getting the basket away from her.

Glancing at it, I thought I saw the lid bulging, but Grandfather had tied it down quite firmly this time and there was little likelihood of its suddenly bursting open.

An enormous taxi was waiting outside the station, and the family tumbled into it. Timothy got on to the back seat, leaving enough room for Grandfather and me. Aunt Emily sat up in front with Grandmother, the tiffin-basket on her lap.

'I'm dying to see what's inside,' she said. 'Can't I take just a little peek?'

'Not now,' said Grandfather. 'First let's enjoy the breakfast you've got waiting for us.'

'Yes, wait until we get home,' said Grandmother. 'Now tell the taxi driver where to take us, dear. He's looking rather nervous.'

Aunt Emily gave instructions to the driver and the taxi shot off in a cloud of dust.

'Well, here we go!' said Grandfather. 'I'm looking forward to having a nice peaceful time here.'

Popeye, perched proudly on Grandmother's shoulder, kept one suspicious eye on the quivering tiffin-basket.

'All aboard!' he squawked. 'All aboard!'

When we got to Aunt Emily's house, we found a light breakfast waiting for us on the dining table.

'It isn't much,' said Aunt Emily. 'But we'll supplement it with the contents of your hamper.' And placing the basket on the table, she removed the lid.

The python was half-asleep, with an apple in its mouth. Aunt Emily was no Eve, to be tempted. She fainted away.

Grandfather promptly picked up the python, took it into the garden, and draped it over a branch of a guava tree.

When Aunt Emily recovered, she insisted that there was a huge snake in the tiffin-basket. We showed her the empty basket.

'You're seeing things,' said Grandfather.

'It must be the heat,' I said.

Grandmother said nothing. But Popeye broke into shrieks of maniacal laughter, and soon everyone, including a slightly hysterical Aunt Emily, was doubled up with laughter.

Escape from Java

IT ALL HAPPENED within the space of a few days. The cassia tree had barely come into flower when the first bombs fell on Batavia (now called Jakarta) and the bright pink blossoms lay scattered over the wreckage in the streets.

News had reached us that Singapore had fallen to the Japanese. My father said: 'I expect it won't be long before they take Java. With the British defeated, how can the Dutch be expected to win!' He did not mean to be critical of the Dutch; he knew they did not have the backing of the Empire that Britain had. Singapore had been called the Gibraltar of the East. After its surrender there could only be retreat, a vast exodus of Europeans from South East Asia.

It was 1940 and the Second World War was on. What the Javanese thought about the war is now hard for me to say, because I was only nine at the time and knew very little of worldly matters. Most people knew they would be exchanging their Dutch rulers for Japanese rulers, but there were also many who spoke in terms of freedom for Java when the war was over.

Our neighbour, Mr Hartono, was one of those who looked ahead to a time when Java, Sumatra and the other islands would make up one independent nation. He was a college professor and spoke Dutch, Chinese, Javanese and a little English. His son, Sono, was about my age. He was the only boy I knew who could talk to me in English, and as a result we spent a lot of time together. Our favourite pastime was flying kites in the park.

The bombing soon put an end to kite flying. Air raid alerts sounded at all hours of the day and night and, although in the beginning most of the bombs fell near the docks, a couple of miles from where we lived, we had to stay indoors. If the planes sounded very near, we dived under beds or tables. I don't remember if there were any trenches. Probably there hadn't been time for trench digging, and now there was time only for digging graves. Events had moved all too swiftly, and everyone (except of course the Javanese) was anxious to get away from Java.

'When are you going?' asked Sono, as we sat on the veranda steps in a pause between air raids.

'I don't know,' I said. 'It all depends on my father.'

'My father says the Japs will be here in a week. And if you're still here then, they'll put you to work building a railway.'

'I wouldn't mind building a railway,' I said.

'But they won't give you enough to eat. Just rice with worms in it. And if you don't work properly, they'll shoot you.'

'They do that to soldiers,' I said. 'We're civilians.'

'They do it to civilians too,' said Sono.

What was I doing in Batavia, when the only homes I had known had been in India—first with my father, and later my paternal grandparents? My father worked for a firm dealing in rubber—his job took him to many places—and six months earlier he had been sent to Batavia to open a new office in partnership with a Dutch business house. I had joined my father in Batavia only four months back. After the war was over he was going to take me to England.

'Are we going to win the war?' I asked.

'It doesn't look like it from here,' he said.

No, it didn't look as though we were winning. Standing at the docks with my father, I watched the ships arrive from Singapore crowded with refugees—men, women and children, all living on the decks in the hot tropical sun; they looked pale and worn-out and worried.

They were on their way to Colombo or Bombay. No one came ashore at Batavia. It wasn't British territory; it was Dutch, and everyone knew it wouldn't be Dutch for long.

'Aren't we going too?' I asked. 'Sono's father says the Japs will be here any day.'

'We've still got a few days,' said my father. He was a short, stocky man, who seldom got excited. If he was worried, he didn't show it. 'I've got to wind up a few business matters, and then we'll be off.'

'How will we go? There's no room for us on those ships.'

'There certainly isn't. But we'll find a way, Rusty, don't worry.'

I didn't worry. I had complete confidence in my father's ability to find a way out of difficulties. He used to say, 'Every problem has a solution hidden away somewhere, and if only you look hard enough you will find it.'

There were British soldiers in the streets but they did not make us feel much safer. They were just waiting for troop ships to come and take them away. No one, it seemed, was interested in defending Java, only in getting out as fast as possible.

Although the Dutch were unpopular with the Javanese people, there was no ill-feeling against individual Europeans. I could walk safely through the streets. Occasionally small boys in the crowded Chinese quarter would point at me and shout, '*Orang Balandi!*' (Dutchman!) but they did so in good humour, and I didn't know the language well enough to stop and explain that the English weren't Dutch. For them, all white people were the same, and understandably so.

My father's office was in the commercial area, along the canal banks. Our two-storeyed house, about a mile away, was an old building with a roof of red tiles and a broad balcony which had stone dragons at either end. There were flowers in the garden almost all the year round. If there was anything in Batavia more regular than the bombing, it was the rain, which came pattering down on the roof and on the banana fronds almost every afternoon. In the hot and steamy atmosphere of Java, the rain was always welcome.

There were no anti-aircraft guns in Batavia—at least we never heard any—and the Jap bombers came over at will, dropping their bombs by daylight. Sometimes bombs fell in the town. One day the building next to my father's office received a direct hit and tumbled into the river. A number of office workers were killed.

The schools closed, and Sono and I had nothing to do all day except sit in the house, playing darts or carrom, wrestling on the carpets, or playing the gramophone. We had records by Gracie Fields, Harry

Lauder, George Formby and Arthur Askey, all popular British artists. One song by Arthur Askey made fun of Adolph Hitler, with the words, 'Adolph, we're gonna hang up your washing on the Siegfried Line, if the Siegfried Line's still there!' It made us feel quite cheerful to know that back in Britain people were confident of winning the war!

One day Sono said, 'The bombs are falling on Batavia, not in the countryside. Why don't we get cycles and ride out of town?'

I fell in with the idea at once. After the morning all-clear had sounded, we mounted our cycles and rode out of town. Mine was a hired cycle, but Sono's was his own. He'd had it since the age of five, and it was constantly in need of repair. 'The soul has gone out of it,' he used to say.

Our fathers were at work; Sono's mother had gone out to do her shopping (during air raids she took shelter under the most convenient shop counter) and wouldn't be back for at least an hour. We expected to be back before lunch.

We were soon out of town, on a road that passed through rice fields, pineapple orchards and cinchona plantations. On our right lay dark green hills, on our left, groves of coconut palms and, beyond them, the sea. Men and women were working in the rice fields, knee-deep in mud, their broad-brimmed hats protecting them from the fierce sun. Here and there a buffalo wallowed in a pool of brown water, while a naked boy lay stretched out on the animal's broad back.

We took a bumpy track through the palms. They grew right down to the edge of the sea. Leaving our cycles on the shingle, we ran down a smooth, sandy beach and into the shallow water.

'Don't go too far in,' warned Sono. 'There may be sharks about.'

Wading in amongst the rocks, we searched for interesting shells, then sat down on a large rock and looked out to sea, where a sailing ship moved placidly on the crisp, blue waters. It was difficult to imagine that half the world was at war, and that Batavia, two or three miles away, was right in the middle of it.

On our way home we decided to take a shortcut through the rice fields, but soon found that our tyres got bogged down in the soft mud. This delayed our return; and to make things worse, we got the roads mixed up and reached an area of the town that seemed unfamiliar. We had barely entered the outskirts when the siren sounded, followed soon after by the drone of an approaching aircraft.

'Should we get off our cycles and take shelter somewhere?' I called out.

'No, let's race home!' shouted Sono. 'The bombs won't fall here.'

But he was wrong. The planes flew in very low. Looking up for a moment, I saw the sun blotted out by the sinister shape of a Jap fighter-bomber. We pedalled furiously; but we had barely covered fifty yards when there was a terrific explosion on our right, behind some houses. The shock sent us spinning across the road. We were flung from our cycles. And the cycles, still propelled by the blast, crashed into a wall.

I felt a stinging sensation in my hands and legs, as though scores of little insects had bitten me. Tiny droplets of blood appeared here and there on my flesh. Sono was on all fours, crawling beside me, and I saw that he too had the same small scratches on his hands and forehead, made by tiny shards of flying glass.

We were quickly on our feet, and then we began running in the general direction of our homes. The twisted cycles lay forgotten on the road.

'Get off the street, you two!' shouted someone from a window; but we weren't going to stop running until we got home. And we ran faster than we'd ever run in our lives.

My father and Sono's parents were themselves

running about the street, calling for us, when we came rushing around the corner and tumbled into their arms.

'Where have you been?'

'What happened to you?'

'How did you get those cuts?'

All superfluous questions but before we could recover our breath and start explaining, we were bundled into our respective homes. My father washed my cuts and scratches and dabbed at my face and legs with iodine—ignoring my yelps—and then stuck plaster all over my face.

Sono and I had had a fright, and we did not venture far from the house again.

That night my father said, 'I think we'll be able to leave in a day or two.'

'Has another ship come in?'

'No.'

'Then how are we going? By plane?'

'Wait and see, Rusty. It isn't settled yet. But we won't be able to take much with us—just enough to fill a couple of travelling bags.'

'What about the stamp collection?' I asked.

My father's stamp collection was quite valuable and filled several volumes.

'I'm afraid we'll have to leave most of it behind,' he said. 'Perhaps Mr Hartono will keep it for me, and when the war is over—if it's over—we'll come back for it.'

'But we can take one or two albums with us, can't we?'

'I'll take one. There'll be room for one. Then if we're short of money in Bombay, we can sell the stamps.'

'Bombay? That's in India. I thought we were going straight to England.'

'First we must go to India.'

The following morning I found Sono in the garden, patched up like me, and with one foot in a bandage. But he was as cheerful as ever and gave me his usual wide grin.

'We're leaving tomorrow,' I said.

The grin left his face.

'I will be sad when you go,' he said. 'But I will be glad too, because then you will be able to escape from the Japs.'

'After the war, I'll come back.'

'Yes, you must come back. And then, when we are big, we will go round the world together. I want to see England and America and Africa and India and Japan. I want to go everywhere.'

'We can't go everywhere.'

'Yes, we can. No one can stop us!'

We had to be up very early the next morning. Our

70

bags had been packed late at night. We were taking a few clothes, some of my father's business papers, a pair of binoculars, one stamp album, and several bars of chocolate. I was pleased about the stamp album and the chocolates, but I had to give up several of my treasures—favourite books, the gramophone and records, an old Samurai sword, a train set and a dartboard. The only consolation was that Sono, and not a stranger, would have them.

In the first faint light of dawn a truck drew up in front of the house. It was driven by a Dutch businessman, Mr Hookens, who worked with my father. Sono was already at the gate, waiting to say goodbye.

'I have a present for you,' he said.

He took me by the hand and pressed a smooth hard object into my palm. I grasped it and then held it up against the light. It was a beautiful little seahorse, carved out of pale blue jade.

'It will bring you luck,' said Sono.

'Thank you,' I said. 'I will keep it forever.'

And I slipped the little seahorse into my pocket.

'In you get, Rusty,' said my father, and I got up on the front seat between him and Mr Hookens.

As the truck started up, I turned to wave to Sono. He was sitting on his garden wall, grinning at me. He called out: 'We will go everywhere, and no one can stop us!'

He was still waving when the truck took us round the bend at the end of the road.

We drove through the still, quiet streets of Batavia, occasionally passing burnt-out trucks and shattered buildings. Then we left the sleeping city far behind and were climbing into the forested hills. It had rained during the night, and when the sun came up over the green hills, it twinkled and glittered on the broad, wet leaves. The light in the forest changed from dark green to greenish gold, broken here and there by the flaming red or orange of a trumpet-shaped blossom. It was impossible to know the names of all those fantastic plants! The road had been cut through dense tropical forest, and on either side the trees jostled each other, hungry for the sun; but they were chained together by the liana creepers and vines that fed upon the struggling trees.

Occasionally a Jelarang, a large Javan squirrel, frightened by the passing of the truck, leapt through the trees before disappearing into the depths of the forest. We saw many birds: peacocks, junglefowl, and once, standing majestically at the side of the road, a crowned pigeon, its great size and splendid crest making it a striking object even at a distance.

Mr Hookens slowed down so that we could look at the bird. It bowed its head so that its crest swept the ground; then it emitted a low hollow boom rather than the call of a turkey.

When we came to a small clearing, we stopped for breakfast. Butterflies, black, green and gold, flitted across the clearing. The silence of the forest was broken only by the drone of airplanes. Japanese Zeros heading for Batavia on another raid. I thought about Sono, and wondered what he would be doing at home: probably trying out the gramophone!

We ate boiled eggs and drank tea from a thermos, then got back into the truck and resumed our journey.

I must have dozed off soon after, because the next thing I remember is that we were going quite fast down a steep, winding road, and in the distance I could see a calm blue lagoon.

'We've reached the sea again,' I said.

'That's right,' said my father. 'But we're now nearly a hundred miles from Batavia, in another part of the island. You're looking out over the Sunda Straits.'

Then he pointed towards a shimmering white object resting on the waters of the lagoon.

'There's our plane,' he said.

'A seaplane!' I exclaimed. 'I never guessed. Where will it take us?'

'To Bombay, I hope. There aren't many other places left to go to!'

It was a very old seaplane, and no one, not even the captain—the pilot was called the captain—could promise that it would take off. Mr Hookens wasn't coming with us; he said the plane would be back for him the next day. Besides my father and me, there were four other passengers, and all but one were Dutch. The odd man out was a Londoner, a motor mechanic who'd been left behind in Java when his unit was evacuated. (He told us later that he'd fallen asleep at a bar in the Chinese quarter, waking up some hours after his regiment had moved off!) He looked rather scruffy. He'd lost the top button of his shirt, but, instead of leaving his collar open, as we did, he'd kept it together with a large safety pin, which thrust itself out from behind a bright pink tie.

'It's a relief to find you here, guvnor,' he said, shaking my father by the hand. 'Knew you for a Yorkshireman the minute I set eyes on you. It's the *song-fried* that does it, if you know what I mean.' (He meant *sang-froid*, French for a 'cool look'.) 'And here I was, with all these flippin' forriners, and me not knowing a word of what they've been yattering about. Do you think this old tub will get us back to Blighty?'

'It does look a bit shaky,' said my father. 'One of

the first flying boats, from the looks of it. If it gets us to Bombay, that's far enough.'

'Anywhere out of Java's good enough for me,' said our new companion. 'The name's Muggeridge.'

'Pleased to know you, Mr Muggeridge,' said my father. 'I'm Bond. This is my son.'

Mr Muggeridge rumpled my hair and favoured me with a large wink.

The captain of the seaplane was beckoning to us to join him in a small skiff which was about to take us across a short stretch of water to the seaplane.

'Here we go,' said Mr Muggeridge. 'Say your prayers and keep your fingers crossed.'

The seaplane was a long time getting airborne. It had to make several runs before it finally took off. Then, lurching drunkenly, it rose into the clear blue sky.

'For a moment I thought we were going to end up in the briny,' said Mr Muggeridge, untying his seat belt. 'And talkin' of fish, I'd give a week's wages for a plate of fish an' chips and a pint of beer.'

'I'll buy you a beer in Bombay,' said my father.

'Have an egg,' I said, remembering we still had some boiled eggs in one of the travelling bags.

'Thanks, mate,' said Mr Muggeridge, accepting an egg with alacrity. 'A real egg, too! I've been livin' on egg powder these last six months. That's what they give you in the Army. And it ain't hens' eggs they make it from, let me tell you. It's either gulls' or turtles' eggs!'

'No,' said my father with a straight face. 'Snakes' eggs.'

Mr Muggeridge turned a delicate shade of green; but he soon recovered his poise, and for about an hour kept talking about almost everything under the sun, including Churchill, Hitler, Roosevelt, Mahatma Gandhi and Betty Grable. (The last named was famous for her beautiful legs.) He would have gone on talking all the way to Bombay had he been given a chance; but suddenly a shudder passed through the old plane, and it began lurching again.

'I think an engine is giving trouble,' said my father.

When I looked through the small glassed-in window, it seemed as though the sea was rushing up to meet us.

The co-pilot entered the passenger cabin and said something in Dutch. The passengers looked dismayed, and immediately began fastening their seat belts.

'Well, what did the blighter say?' asked Mr Muggeridge.

'I think he's going to have to ditch the plane,' said my father, who knew enough Dutch to get the gist of anything that was said.

'Down in the drink!' exclaimed Mr Muggeridge. 'Gawd 'elp us! And how far are we from Bombay, guv?'

'A few hundred miles,' said my father.

'Can you swim, mate?' asked Mr Muggeridge looking at me.

'Yes,' I said. 'But not all the way to Bombay. How far can you swim?'

'The length of a bathtub,' he said.

'Don't worry,' said my father. 'Just make sure your life jacket's properly tied.'

We looked to our life jackets; my father checked mine twice, making sure that it was properly fastened.

The pilot had now cut both engines, and was bringing the plane down in a circling movement. But he couldn't control the speed, and it was tilting heavily to one side. Instead of landing smoothly on its belly, it came down on a wingtip, and this caused the plane to swivel violently around in the choppy sea. There was a terrific jolt when the plane hit the water, and if it hadn't been for the seat belts we'd have been flung from our seats. Even so, Mr Muggeridge struck his head against the seat in front, and was now holding a bleeding nose and using some shocking language.

As soon as the plane came to a standstill, my father undid my seat belt. There was no time to lose. Water was already filling the cabin, and all the passengers— except one, who was dead in his seat with a broken neck—were scrambling for the exit hatch. The co-pilot pulled a lever and the door fell away to reveal high waves slapping against the sides of the stricken plane.

Holding me by the hand, my father was leading me towards the exit.

'Quick, Rusty,' he said. 'We won't stay afloat for long.'

'Give us a hand!' shouted Mr Muggeridge, still struggling with his life jacket. 'First this bloody bleedin' nose, and now something's gone and stuck.'

My father helped him fix the life jacket, then pushed him out of the door ahead of us.

As we swam away from the seaplane (Mr Muggeridge splashing fiercely alongside us), we were aware of the other passengers in the water. One of them shouted to us in Dutch to follow him.

We swam after him towards the dinghy, which had been released the moment we hit the water. That yellow dinghy, bobbing about on the waves, was as welcome as land.

All who had left the plane managed to climb into the dinghy. We were seven altogether—a tight fit. We had hardly settled down in the well of the dinghy when Mr Muggeridge, still holding his nose, exclaimed: 'There she goes!' And as we looked on helplessly, the seaplane sank swiftly and silently beneath the waves.

The dinghy had shipped a lot of water, and soon everyone was busy bailing it out with mugs (there were a couple in the dinghy), hats and bare hands. There was a light swell, and every now and then water would roll in again and half fill the dinghy. But within half an hour we had most of the water out, and then it was possible to take turns, two men doing the bailing while the others rested. No one expected me to do this work, but I gave a hand anyway, using my father's sola topi for the purpose.

'Where are we?' asked one of the passengers.

'A long way from anywhere,' said another.

'There must be a few islands in the Indian Ocean.'

'But we may be at sea for days before we come to one of them.'

'Days or even weeks,' said the captain. 'Let us look at our supplies.'

The dinghy appeared to be fairly well provided with emergency rations: biscuits, raisins, chocolates (we'd lost our own), and enough water to last a week. There was also a first-aid box, which was put to immediate use, as Mr Muggeridge's nose needed attention. A few others had cuts and bruises. One of the passengers had received a hard knock on the head and appeared to be suffering from a loss of memory. He had no idea how we happened to be drifting about in the middle of the Indian Ocean; he was convinced that we were on a pleasure cruise a few miles off Batavia.

The unfamiliar motion of the dinghy, as it rose and fell in the troughs between the waves, resulted in almost everyone getting seasick. As no one could eat anything, a day's rations were saved.

The sun was very hot, but my father covered my head with a large spotted handkerchief. He'd always had a fancy for bandanna handkerchiefs with yellow spots, and seldom carried fewer than two on his person; so he had one for himself too. The sola topi, well soaked in seawater, was being used by Mr Muggeridge.

It was only when I had recovered to some extent from my seasickness that I remembered the valuable stamp album, and sat up, exclaiming, 'The stamps! Did you bring the stamp album, Dad?'

He shook his head ruefully. 'It must be at the bottom of the sea by now. But don't worry, I kept a few rare stamps in my wallet.' And looking pleased with himself, he tapped the pocket of his bush shirt.

The dinghy drifted all day, with no one having the least idea where it might be taking us.

'Probably going round in circles,' said Mr Muggeridge pessimistically.

There was no compass and no sail, and paddling

wouldn't have got us far even if we'd had paddles; we could only resign ourselves to the whims of the current and hope it would take us towards land or at least to within hailing distance of some passing ship.

The sun went down like an overripe tomato dissolving slowly in the sea. The darkness pressed down on us. It was a moonless night, and all we could see was the white foam on the crests of the waves. I lay with my head on my father's shoulder, and looked up at the stars which glittered in the remote heavens.

'Perhaps your friend Sono will look up at the sky tonight and see those same stars,' said my father. 'The world isn't so big after all.'

'All the same, there's a lot of sea around us,' said Mr Muggeridge from out of the darkness.

Remembering Sono, I put my hand into my pocket and was reassured to feel the smooth outline of the jade seahorse.

'I've still got Sono's seahorse,' I said, showing it to my father.

'Keep it carefully,' he said. 'It may bring us luck.'

'Are seahorses lucky?'

'Who knows? But he gave it to you with love, and love is like a prayer. So keep it carefully.'

I didn't sleep much that night. I don't think anyone slept. No one spoke much either, except of course Mr

Muggeridge who kept muttering something about cold beer and salami.

I didn't feel so sick the next day. By ten o'clock I was quite hungry; but breakfast consisted of two biscuits, a piece of chocolate, and a little drinking water. It was another hot day, and we were soon very thirsty, but everyone agreed that we should ration ourselves strictly.

Two or three still felt ill, but the others, including Mr Muggeridge, had recovered their appetites and normal spirits, and there was some discussion about the prospects of being picked up.

'Are there any distress rockets in the dinghy?' asked my father. 'If we see a ship or a plane, we can fire a rocket and hope to be spotted. Otherwise there's not much chance of our being seen from a distance.'

A thorough search was made in the dinghy, but there were no rockets.

'Someone must have used them last Guy Fawkes Day,' commented Mr Muggeridge.

'They don't celebrate Guy Fawkes Day in Holland,' said my father. 'Guy Fawkes was an Englishman.'

'Ah,' said Mr Muggeridge, not in the least put out. 'I've always said, most great men are Englishmen. And what did this chap Guy Fawkes do?'

'Tried to blow up Parliament,' replied my father.

That afternoon we saw our first sharks. They were

enormous creatures, and as they glided backward and forward under the boat it seemed they might hit and capsize us. They went away for some time, but returned in the evening.

At night, as I lay half asleep beside my father, I felt a few drops of water strike my face. At first I thought it was the sea spray; but when the sprinkling continued, I realized that it was raining lightly.

'Rain!' I shouted, sitting up. 'It's raining!'

Everyone woke up and did their best to collect water in mugs, hats or other containers. Mr Muggeridge lay back with his mouth open, drinking the rain as it fell.

'This is more like it,' he said. 'You can have all the sun an' sand in the world. Give me a rainy day in England!'

But by early morning the clouds had passed, and the day turned out to be even hotter than the previous one. Soon we were all red and raw from sunburn. By midday even Mr Muggeridge was silent. No one had the energy to talk.

Then my father whispered, 'Can you hear a plane, Rusty?'

I listened carefully, and above the hiss of the waves I heard what sounded like the distant drone of a plane; but it must have been very far away, because we could not see it. Perhaps it was flying into the sun, and the glare was too much for our sore eyes, or perhaps we'd just imagined the sound.

Then the Dutchman who'd lost his memory thought he saw land, and kept pointing towards the horizon and saying, 'That's Batavia, I told you we were close to shore!' No one else saw anything. So my father and I weren't the only ones imagining things.

Said my father, 'It only goes to show that a man can see what he wants to see, even if there's nothing to be seen!'

The sharks were still with us. Mr Muggeridge began to resent them. He took off one of his shoes and hurled it at the nearest shark; but the big fish ignored the shoe and swam on after us.

'Now, if your leg had been in that shoe, Mr Muggeridge, the shark might have accepted it,' observed my father.

'Don't throw your shoes away,' said the captain. 'We might land on a deserted coastline and have to walk hundreds of miles!'

A light breeze sprang up that evening, and the dinghy moved more swiftly on the choppy water.

'At last we're moving forward,' said the captain.

'In circles,' said Mr Muggeridge.

But the breeze was refreshing; it cooled our burning

limbs, and helped us to get some sleep. In the middle of the night I woke up feeling very hungry.

'Are you all right?' asked my father, who had been awake all the time.

'Just hungry,' I said.

'And what would you like to eat?'

'Oranges!'

He laughed. 'No oranges on board. But I kept a piece of my chocolate for you. And there's a little water, if you're thirsty.'

I kept the chocolate in my mouth for a long time, trying to make it last. Then I sipped a little water.

'Aren't you hungry?' I asked.

'Ravenous! I could eat a whole turkey. When we get to Bombay or Madras or Colombo, or wherever it is we get to, we'll go to the best restaurant in town and eat like—like—'

'Like shipwrecked sailors!' I said.

'Exactly.'

'Do you think we'll ever get to land, Dad?'

'I'm sure we will. You're not afraid, are you?'

'No. Not as long as you're with me.'

Next morning, to everyone's delight, we saw seagulls. This was a sure sign that land couldn't be far away; but a dinghy could take days to drift a distance of thirty or forty miles. The birds wheeled noisily above the dinghy. Their cries were the first familiar sounds we had heard for three days and three nights, apart from the wind and the sea and our own weary voices.

The sharks had disappeared, and that too was an encouraging sign. They didn't like the oil slicks that were appearing in the water.

But presently the gulls left us, and we feared we were drifting away from land.

'Circles,' repeated Mr Muggeridge. 'Circles.'

We had sufficient food and water for another week at sea; but no one even wanted to think about spending another week at sea.

The sun was a ball of fire. Our water ration wasn't sufficient to quench our thirst. By noon, we were without much hope or energy.

My father had his pipe in his mouth. He didn't have any tobacco, but he liked holding the pipe between his teeth. He said it prevented his mouth from getting too dry.

The sharks came back.

Mr Muggeridge removed his other shoe and threw it at them.

'Nothing like a lovely wet English summer,' he mumbled.

I fell asleep in the well of the dinghy, my father's large handkerchief spread over my face. The yellow spots on the cloth seemed to grow into enormous revolving suns.

When I woke up, I found a huge shadow hanging over us. At first I thought it was a cloud. But it was a shifting shadow. My father took the handkerchief from my face and said, 'You can wake up now, Rusty. We'll be home and dry soon.'

A fishing boat was beside us, and the shadow came from its wide, flapping sail. A number of bronzed, smiling, chattering fishermen were gazing down at us from the deck of their boat.

A few days later my father and I were in Bombay.

My father sold his rare stamps for over a thousand rupees, and we were able to live in a comfortable hotel.

Mr Muggeridge was flown back to England. Later we got a postcard from him, saying the English rain was awful!

Meanwhile, I had the jade seahorse which Sono had given me.

And I have it with me today.

The Room of
Many Colours

THERE WAS THIS red insect, just like a velvet button, which I found on the front lawn of the bungalow. The grass was still wet with overnight rain.

I placed the insect on the palm of my hand and took it into the house to show my father.

'Look, Dad,' I said, 'I haven't seen an insect like this before. Where has it come from?'

'Where did you find it?' he asked.

'On the grass.'

'It must have come down from the sky,' he said. 'It must have come down with the rain.'

Later, he told me how the insect really happened but I preferred his first explanation. It was more fun to have it dropping from the sky.

I was nine at the time, and my father was thirty-nine, but, right from the beginning, he made me feel that I was old enough to talk to him about everything—insects, people, trees, steam engines, King George, comics, crocodiles, the Mahatma, the Viceroy, America, Mozambique and Timbuctoo. We took long walks together, explored old ruins, chased butterflies and waved to passing trains.

We were sitting on an old wall, looking out to sea at a couple of Arab dhows and a tram steamer, when my father said, 'Would you like to go to sea one day?'

'Where does the sea go?' I asked.

'It goes everywhere.'

'Does it go to the end of the world?'

'It goes right round the world. It's a round world.'

'It can't be.'

'It is. But it's so big, you can't see the roundness. When a fly sits on a watermelon, it can't see right round the melon, can it? The melon must seem quite flat to the fly. Well, in comparison to the world, we're much, much smaller than the tiniest of insects.'

'Have you been around the world?' I asked.

'No, only as far as England. That's where your grandfather was born.'

'And my grandmother?'

'She is British too, though she came to India from Norway when she was quite small. Norway is a cold land, with mountains and snow, and the sea cutting deep into the land. Your grandparents took me over there for a visit when I was a boy. It's very beautiful, and the people are good and work hard.'

'I'd like to go there.'

'You will, one day. When you are older, I'll take you to Norway.'

'Is it better than England?'

'It's quite different.'

'Is it better than India?'

'It's quite different.'

'Is India like England?'

'No, it's different.'

'Well, what does "different" mean?'

'It means things are not the same. It means people are different. It means the weather is different. It means trees and birds and insects found in each of these places are different.'

'Are English crocodiles different from Indian crocodiles?'

'They don't have crocodiles in England.'

'Oh, then it must be different.'

'It would be a dull world if it was the same everywhere, Rusty,' said my father.

He never lost patience with my endless questioning. If he wanted a rest, he would take out his pipe and spend a long time lighting it. If this took very long, I'd find something else to do. But sometimes I'd wait patiently until the pipe was drawing, and then return to the attack.

'Will we always be in India?' I asked.

'No, we'll have to go away one day. You see, it's hard to explain, but it isn't really our country.'

'Ayah says it belongs to the King of England, and the jewels in his crown were taken from India, and that when the Indians get their jewels back, the King will lose India! But first they have to get the crown from the King, but this is very difficult, she says, because the crown is always on his head. He even sleeps wearing his crown!'

Ayah was my nanny. She loved me deeply, and was always filling my head with strange and wonderful stories.

My father did not comment on Ayah's views. All he said was, 'We'll have to go away some day.'

'How long have we been here?' I asked.

'Two hundred years.'

'No, I mean *us*.'

'Well, I was born in India and so were you, so that's thirty-nine years.'

'Then can't I stay here?'

'Do you want to?'

'I want to go across the sea. But can we take Ayah with us?'

'I don't know, son. Let's walk along the beach.'

We lived in an old palace beside a lake. The palace looked like a ruin from the outside, but the rooms were cool and comfortable. We lived in one wing, and my father organized a small school in another wing. His pupils were the children of the Raja and the Raja's relatives. The pay wasn't much, but we had a palace to live in, the latest 1940-model Hillman to drive about in, and a number of servants. In those days, of course, everyone had servants (although the servants did not have any!). Ayah was our own; but the cook, the bearer, the gardener and the *bhisti* were all provided by the state.

Sometimes I sat in the schoolroom with the other children (who were all much bigger than me), sometimes I remained in the house with Ayah, sometimes I followed the gardener, Dukhi, about the spacious garden.

Dukhi means 'sad', and though I never could discover if the gardener had anything to feel sad about, the name certainly suited him. He had grown to resemble the drooping weeds that he was always digging up with a tiny spade. I seldom saw him standing up. He always sat on the ground with his knees well up to his chin, and attacked the weeds from this position. He could spend all day on his haunches, moving about the garden simply by shuffling his feet along the grass. He reminded me of Govind—the gardener who worked for my grandparents at their home in Dehra.

I tried to imitate Dukhi's posture, sitting down on my heels and drawing up my knees into my armpits, but could never hold the position for more than five minutes.

Time had no meaning in a large garden, and Dukhi never hurried. Life, for him, was not a matter of one year succeeding another, but of five seasons—winter, spring, hot weather, monsoon and autumn—arriving and departing. His seedbeds always had to be in readiness for the coming season, and he did not look any further than the next monsoon. It was impossible to tell his age. He may have been thirty-six or eighty-six. He was either very young for his years or very old for them.

Dukhi loved bright colours, specially reds and yellows. He liked strongly scented flowers, like jasmine and honeysuckle. He couldn't understand my father's preference for the more delicately perfumed petunias and sweet peas. But I shared Dukhi's fondness for the common bright orange marigold, which is offered in temples and is used to make garlands and nosegays.

When the garden was bare of all colour, the marigold would still be there, gay and flashy, challenging the sun.

Dukhi was very fond of making nosegays, and I liked to watch him at work. A sunflower formed the centrepiece. It was surrounded by roses, marigolds and oleander, fringed with green leaves, and bound together with silver thread. The perfume was overpowering. The nosegays were presented to me or my father on special occasions, that is, on a birthday or to guests of my father's who were considered important.

One day I found Dukhi making a nosegay, and said, 'No one is coming today, Dukhi. It isn't even a birthday.'

'It is a birthday, chhota sahib,' he said. 'Little sahib' was the title he had given me. It wasn't much of a title compared to Raja sahib, Diwan sahib or Burra sahib, but it was nice to have a title at the age of nine.

'Oh,' I said. 'And is there a party too?'

'No party.'

'What's the use of a birthday without a party? What's the use of a birthday without presents?'

'This person doesn't like presents—just flowers.'

'Who is it?' I asked, full of curiosity.

'If you want to find out, you can take these flowers to her. She lives right at the top of that far side of the palace. There are twenty-two steps to climb. Remember that, chhota sahib, you take twenty-three steps and you will go over the edge and into the lake!'

I started climbing the stairs.

It was a spiral staircase of wrought iron, and it went round and round and up and up, and it made me quite dizzy and tired.

At the top, I found myself on a small balcony which looked out over the lake and another palace, at the crowded city and the distant harbour. I heard a voice, a rather high, musical voice, saying (in English), 'Are you a ghost?' I turned to see who had spoken but found the balcony empty. The voice had come from a dark room.

I turned to the stairway, ready to flee, but the voice said, 'Oh, don't go, there's nothing to be frightened of!'

And so I stood still, peering cautiously into the darkness of the room.

'First, tell me—are you a ghost?'

'I'm a boy,' I said.

'And I'm a girl. We can be friends. I can't come out there, so you had better come in. Come along, I'm not a ghost either—not yet, anyway!'

As there was nothing very frightening about the voice, I stepped into the room. It was dark inside, and, coming in from the glare, it took me some time to make out the tiny, elderly lady seated on a cushioned gilt chair. She wore a red sari, lots of coloured bangles on her wrists, and golden earrings. Her hair was streaked with white, but her skin was still quite smooth and unlined, and she had large and very beautiful eyes.

'You must be Master Bond!' she said. 'Do you know who I am?'

'You're a person with a birthday,' I said, 'but that's all I know. Dukhi didn't tell me any more.'

'If you promise to keep it secret, I'll tell you who I am. You see, everyone thinks I'm mad. Do you think so too?'

'I don't know.'

'Well, you must tell me if you think so,' she said with a chuckle. Her laugh was the sort of sound made by the gecko, a little wall-lizard, coming from deep down in the throat. 'I have a feeling you are a truthful boy. Do you find it very difficult to tell the truth?'

'Sometimes.'

'Sometimes. Of course, there are times when I tell lies—lots of little lies—because they're such fun! But would you call me a liar? I wouldn't, if I were you, but *would* you?'

'Are you a liar?'

'I'm asking you! If I were to tell you that I was a queen—that I *am* a queen—would you believe me?'

97

I thought deeply about this, and then said, 'I'll try to believe you.'

'Oh, but you *must* believe me. I'm a real queen, I'm a Rani! Look, I've got diamonds to prove it!' And she held out her hands, and there was a ring on each finger, the stones glowing and glittering in the dim light. 'Diamonds, rubies, pearls and emeralds! Only a queen can have these!' She was most anxious that I should believe her.

'You must be a queen,' I said.

'Right!' she snapped. 'In that case, would you mind calling me "Your Highness"?'

'Your Highness,' I said.

She smiled. It was a slow, beautiful smile. Her whole face lit up.

'I could love you,' she said. 'But better still, I'll give you something to eat. Do you like chocolates?'

'Yes, Your Highness.'

'Well,' she said, taking a box from the table beside her, 'these have come all the way from England. Take two. Only two, mind, otherwise the box will finish before Thursday, and I don't want that to happen because I won't get any more till Saturday. That's when Captain MacWhirr's ship gets in, the *S.S. Lucy*, loaded with boxes and boxes of chocolates!'

'All for you?' I asked in considerable awe.

'Yes, of course. They have to last at least three months. I get them from England. I get only the best chocolates. I like them with pink, crunchy fillings, don't you?'

'Oh, yes!' I exclaimed, full of envy.

'Never mind,' she said. 'I may give you one now and then—if you're very nice to me! Here you are, help yourself . . .' She pushed the chocolate box towards me.

I took a silver-wrapped chocolate, and then just as I was thinking of taking a second, she quickly took the box away.

'No more!' she said. 'They have to last till Saturday.'

'But I took only *one*,' I said with some indignation.

'Did you?' She gave me a sharp look, decided I was telling the truth, and said graciously, 'Well, in that case, you can have another.'

Watching the Rani carefully, in case she snatched the box away again, I selected a second chocolate, this one with a green wrapper. I don't remember what kind of day it was outside, but I remember the bright green of the chocolate wrapper.

I thought it would be rude to eat the chocolates in front of a queen, so I put them in my pocket and said, 'I'd better go now. Ayah will be looking for me.'

'And when will you be coming to see me again?'

'I don't know,' I said.

'Your Highness.'

'Your Highness.'

'There's something I want you to do for me,' she said, placing one finger on my shoulder and giving me a conspiratorial look. 'Will you do it?'

'What is it, Your Highness?'

'What is it? Why do you ask? A real prince never asks where or why or whatever, he simply does what the princess asks of him. When I was a princess— before I became a queen, that is—I asked a prince to swim across the lake and fetch me a lily growing on the other bank.'

'And did he get it for you?'

'He drowned halfway across. Let *that* be a lesson to you. Never agree to do something without knowing what it is.'

'But I thought you said . . .'

'Never mind what I *said*. It's what I *say* that matters!'

'Oh, all right,' I said, fidgeting to be gone. 'What is it you want me to do?'

'Nothing.' Her tiny rosebud lips pouted and she stared sullenly at a picture on the wall. Now that my eyes had grown used to the dim light in the room, I noticed that the walls were hung with portraits of stout Rajas and Ranis turbaned and bedecked in fine clothes. There were also portraits of Queen Victoria and King George V of England. And, in the centre of all this distinguished company, a large picture of Mickey Mouse.

'I'll do it if it isn't too dangerous,' I said.

'Then listen.' She took my hand and drew me towards her—what a tiny hand she had!—and whispered, 'I want a *red* rose. From the palace garden. But be careful! Don't let Dukhi, the gardener, catch you. He'll know it's for me. He knows I love roses. And he hates me! I'll tell you why, one day. But if he catches you, he'll do something terrible.'

'To me?'

'No, to himself. That's much worse, isn't it? He'll tie himself into knots, or lie naked on a bed of thorns, or go on a long fast with nothing to eat but fruit, sweets and chicken! So you will be careful, won't you?'

'Oh, but he doesn't hate you,' I cried in protest, remembering the flowers he'd sent for her, and looking around I found that I'd been sitting on them. 'Look, he sent these flowers for your birthday!'

'Well, if he sent them for my birthday, you can take them back,' she snapped. 'But if he sent them for *me* . . .' and she suddenly softened and looked coy, 'then I might keep them. Thank you, my dear, it was a very sweet thought.' And she leant forward as though to kiss me.

'It's late, I must go!' I said in alarm, and turning on my heels, ran out of the room and down the spiral staircase.

Father hadn't started lunch, or rather tiffin, as we called it then. He usually waited for me if I was late. I don't suppose he enjoyed eating alone.

For tiffin, we usually had rice, a mutton curry (koftas or meatballs, with plenty of gravy, was my favourite curry), fried dal and a hot lime or mango pickle. For supper, we had English food—a soup, roast pork and fried potatoes, a rich gravy made by my father, and a custard or caramel pudding. My father enjoyed cooking, but it was only in the morning that he found time for it. Breakfast was his own creation. He cooked eggs in a variety of interesting ways, and favoured some Italian recipes which he had collected from some cookbook belonging to Grandmother.

In deference to the feelings of our Hindu friends, we did not eat beef; but, apart from mutton and chicken, there was a plentiful supply of other meats—partridge, venison, lobster, and even porcupine!

'And where have you been?' asked my father, helping himself to the rice as soon as he saw me come in.

'To the top of the old palace,' I said.

'Did you meet anyone there?'

'Yes, I met a tiny lady who told me she was a Rani. She gave me chocolates.'

'As a rule, she doesn't like visitors.'

'Oh, she didn't mind me. But is she really a queen?'

'Well, she's the daughter of a Maharaja. That makes her a princess. She never married. There's a story that she fell in love with a commoner, one of the palace servants, and wanted to marry him, but of course they wouldn't allow that. She became very melancholic, and started living all by herself in the old palace. They give her everything she needs, but she doesn't go out or have visitors. Everyone says she's mad.'

'How do they know?' I asked.

'Because she's different from other people, I suppose.'

'Is that being mad?'

'No. Not really, I suppose, madness is not *seeing* things as others see them.'

'Is that very bad?'

'No,' said Father, who for once was finding it very difficult to explain something to me. 'But people who are like that—people whose minds are so different that they don't think, step by step, as we do, whose thoughts jump all over the place—such people are very difficult to live with.'

'Step by step,' I repeated. 'Step by step . . .'

'You aren't eating,' said my father. 'Hurry up, and you can come with me to school today.'

I always looked forward to attending my father's classes. He did not take me to the schoolroom very often, because he wanted school to be a treat, to begin with, and then, later, the routine wouldn't be so unwelcome.

Sitting there with older children, understanding only half of what they were learning, I felt important and part grown up. And of course I did learn to read and write, although I first learnt to read upside down, by means of standing in front of the others' desks and peering across at their books. Later, when I went to school, I had some difficulty in learning to read the right way up; and even today I sometimes read upside down, for the sake of variety. I don't mean that I read standing on my head, simply that I hold the book upside down.

I had at my command a number of rhymes and jingles, the most interesting of these being 'Solomon Grundy'.

Solomon Grundy,
Born on a Monday,
Christened on Tuesday,

Married on Wednesday,
Took ill on Thursday,
Worse on Friday,
Died on Saturday,
Buried on Sunday:
This is the end of
Solomon Grundy.

Was that all that life amounted to, in the end? And were we all Solomon Grundies? These were questions that bothered me at the time.

Another puzzling rhyme was the one that went:

Hark, hark,
The dogs do bark,
The beggars are coming to town;
Some in rags,
Some in bags,
And some in velvet gowns.

This rhyme puzzled me for a long time. There were beggars aplenty in the bazaar, and sometimes they came to the house, and some of them did wear rags and bags (and some nothing at all) and the dogs did bark at them, but the beggar in the velvet gown never came our way.

'Who's this beggar in a velvet gown?' I asked my father.

'Not a beggar at all,' he said.

'Then why call him one?'

And I went to Ayah and asked her the same question, 'Who is the beggar in the velvet gown?'

'Jesus Christ,' said Ayah.

Ayah was a fervent Christian and made me say my prayers at night, even when I was very sleepy. She had, I think, Arab and Negro blood in addition to the blood of the Koli fishing community to which her mother had belonged. Her father, a sailor on an Arab dhow, had been a convert to Christianity. Ayah was a large, buxom woman, with heavy hands and feet and a slow, swaying gait that had all the grace and majesty of a royal elephant. Elephants for all their size are nimble creatures; and Ayah, too, was nimble, sensitive, and gentle with her big hands. Her face was always sweet and childlike.

Although a Christian, she clung to many of the beliefs of her parents, and loved to tell me stories about mischievous spirits and evil spirits, humans who changed into animals, and snakes who had been princes in their former lives.

There was the story of the snake who married a princess. At first the princess did not wish to marry the snake, whom she had met in a forest, but the snake insisted, saying, 'I'll kill you if you won't marry me,' and of course that settled the question. The snake led his bride away and took her to a great treasure. 'I was a prince in my former life,' he explained. 'This treasure is yours.' And then the snake very gallantly disappeared.

'Snakes,' declared Ayah, 'are very lucky omens if seen early in the morning.'

'But what if the snake bites the lucky person?' I asked.

'He will be lucky all the same,' said Ayah with a logic that was all her own.

Snakes! There were a number of them living in the big garden, and my father had advised me to avoid the long grass. But I had seen snakes crossing the road (a lucky omen, according to Ayah) and they were never aggressive.

'A snake won't attack you,' said Father, 'provided you leave it alone. Of course, if you step on one, it will probably bite.'

'Are all snakes poisonous?'

'Yes, but only a few are poisonous enough to kill a man. Others use their poison on rats and frogs. A good thing, too, otherwise during the rains the house would be taken over by the frogs.'

One afternoon, while Father was at school, Ayah found a snake in the bathtub. It wasn't early morning and so the snake couldn't have been a lucky one. Ayah was frightened and ran into the garden calling for help. Dukhi came running. Ayah ordered me to stay outside while they went after the snake.

And it was while I was alone in the garden—an unusual circumstance, since Dukhi was nearly always there—that I remembered the Rani's request. On an impulse, I went to the nearest rose bush and plucked the largest rose, pricking my thumb in the process.

And then, without waiting to see what had happened to the snake (it finally escaped), I started up the steps to the top of the old palace.

When I got to the top, I knocked on the door of the Rani's room. Getting no reply, I walked along the balcony until I reached another doorway. There were wooden panels around the door, with elephants, camels and turbaned warriors carved into it. As the door was open, I walked boldly into the room, then stood still in astonishment. The room was filled with a strange light.

There were windows going right round the room, and each small windowpane was made of a different coloured glass. The sun that came through one window flung red and green and purple colours on the figure of the little Rani who stood there with her face pressed to the glass.

She spoke to me without turning from the window.

'This is my favourite room. I have all the colours here. I can see a different world through each pane of glass. Come, join me!' And she beckoned to me, her small hand fluttering like a delicate butterfly.

I went up to the Rani. She was only a little taller than me, and we were able to share the same windowpane.

'See, it's a red world!' she said.

The garden below, the palace and the lake were all tinted red. I watched the Rani's world for a little while and then touched her on the arm and said, 'I have brought you a rose!'

She started away from me, and her eyes looked frightened. She would not look at the rose.

'Oh, why did you bring it?' she cried, wringing her hands. 'He'll be arrested now!'

'Who'll be arrested?'

'The prince, of course!'

'But *I* took it,' I said. 'No one saw me. Ayah and Dukhi were inside the house, catching a snake.'

'Did they catch it?' she asked, forgetting about the rose.

'I don't know. I didn't wait to see!'

'They should follow the snake, instead of catching it. It may lead them to a treasure. All snakes have treasures to guard.'

This seemed to confirm what Ayah had been telling

me, and I resolved that I would follow the next snake that I met.

'Don't you like the rose, then?' I asked.

'Did you steal it?'

'Yes.'

'Good. Flowers should always be stolen. They're more fragrant that way.'

Because of a man called Hitler, war had been declared in Europe and Britain was fighting Germany.

In the comics in the papers, the Germans were usually shown as blundering idiots; so I didn't see how Britain could possibly lose the war, nor why it should concern India, nor why it should be necessary for my father to join up. But I remember him showing me a newspaper headline which said:

BOMBS FALL ON BUCKINGHAM PALACE-KING AND QUEEN SAFE

I expect that had something to do with it.

He went to Delhi for an interview with the RAF and I was left in Ayah's charge.

It was a week I remember well, because it was the first time I had been left on my own. That first night I was afraid—afraid of the dark, afraid of the emptiness of the house, afraid of the howling of the jackals outside.

The loud ticking of the clock was the only reassuring sound: clocks really made themselves heard in those days! I tried concentrating on the ticking, shutting out other sounds and the menace of the dark, but it wouldn't work. I thought I heard a faint hissing near the bed, and sat up, bathed in perspiration, certain that a snake was in the room. I shouted for Ayah and she came running, switching on all the lights.

'A snake!' I cried. 'There's a snake in the room!'

'Where, baba?'

'I don't know where, but I *heard* it.'

Ayah looked under the bed, and behind the chairs and tables, but there was no snake to be found. She persuaded me that I must have heard the breeze whispering in the mosquito curtains.

But I didn't want to be left alone.

'I'm coming to you,' I said and followed her into her small room near the kitchen.

Ayah slept on a low string cot. The mattress was thin, the blanket worn and patched up; but Ayah's warm and solid body made up for the discomfort of the bed. I snuggled up to her and was soon asleep.

I had almost forgotten the Rani in the old palace and was about to pay her a visit when, to my surprise, I found her in the garden.

I had risen early that morning, and had gone

running barefoot over the dew-drenched grass. No one was about, but I startled a flock of parrots and the birds rose screeching from a banyan tree and wheeled away to some other corner of the palace grounds. I was just in time to see a mongoose scurrying across the grass with an egg in its mouth. The mongoose must have been raiding the poultry farm at the palace.

I was trying to locate the mongoose's hideout, and was on all fours in a jungle of tall cosmos plants when I heard the rustle of clothes, and turned to find the Rani staring at me.

She didn't ask me what I was doing there, but simply said, 'I don't think he could have gone in there.'

'But I saw him go this way,' I said.

'Nonsense! He doesn't live in this part of the garden. He lives in the roots of the banyan tree.'

'But that's where the snake lives,' I said

'You mean the snake who was a prince. Well, that's who I'm looking for!'

'A snake who was a prince!' I gaped at the Rani.

She made a gesture of impatience with her butterfly hands, and said, 'Tut, you're only a child, you can't *understand*. The prince lives in the roots of the banyan tree, but he comes out early every morning. Have you seen him?'

'No. But I saw a mongoose.'

The Rani became frightened. 'Oh dear, is there a mongoose in the garden? He might kill the prince!'

'How can a mongoose kill a prince?' I asked.

'You don't understand, Master Bond. Princes, when they die, are born again as snakes.'

'*All* princes?'

'No, only those who die before they can marry.'

'Did your prince die before he could marry you?'

'Yes. And he returned to this garden in the form of a beautiful snake.'

'Well,' I said, 'I hope it wasn't the snake the water-carrier killed last week.'

'He killed a snake!' The Rani looked horrified. She was quivering all over. 'It might have been the prince!'

'It was a brown snake,' I said.

'Oh, then it wasn't him.' She looked very relieved. 'Brown snakes are only ministers and people like that. It has to be a green snake to be a prince.'

'I haven't seen any green snakes here.'

'There's one living in the roots of the banyan tree. You won't kill it, will you?'

'Not if it's really a prince.'

'And you won't let others kill it?'

'I'll tell Ayah.'

'Good. You're on my side. But be careful of the gardener. Keep him away from the banyan tree. He's

113

always killing snakes. I don't trust him at all.'

She came nearer and, leaning forward a little, looked into my eyes.

'Blue eyes—I trust them. But don't trust green eyes. And yellow eyes are evil.'

'I've never seen yellow eyes.'

'That's because you're pure,' she said, and turned away and hurried across the lawn as though she had just remembered a very urgent appointment.

The sun was up, slanting through the branches of the banyan tree, and Ayah's voice could be heard calling me for breakfast.

'Dukhi,' I said, when I found him in the garden later that day, 'Dukhi, don't kill the snake in the banyan tree.'

'A snake in the banyan tree!' he exclaimed, seizing his hoe.

'No, no!' I said. 'I haven't seen it. But the Rani says there's one. She says it was a prince in its former life, and that we shouldn't kill it.'

'Oh,' said Dukhi, smiling to himself. 'The Rani says so. All right, you tell her we won't kill it.'

'Is it true that she was in love with a prince but that he died before she could marry him?'

'Something like that,' said Dukhi. 'It was a long time ago—before I came here.'

'My father says it wasn't a prince, but a commoner. Are you a commoner, Dukhi?'

'A commoner? What's that, chhota sahib?'

'I'm not sure. Someone very poor, I suppose.'

'Then I must be a commoner,' said Dukhi.

'Were *you* in love with the Rani?' I asked.

Dukhi was so startled that he dropped his hoe and lost his balance, the first time I'd seen him lose his poise while squatting on his haunches.

'Don't say such things, chhota sahib!'

'Why not?'

'You'll get me into trouble.'

'Then it must be true.'

Dukhi threw up his hands in mock despair and started collecting his implements.

'It's true, it's true!' I cried, dancing round him, and then I ran indoors to Ayah and said, 'Ayah, Dukhi was in love with the Rani!'

Ayah gave a shriek of laughter, then looked very serious and put her finger against my lips.

'Don't say such things,' she said. 'Dukhi is of a very low caste. People won't like it if they hear what you say. And besides, the Rani told you her prince died and turned into a snake. Well, Dukhi hasn't become a snake as yet, has he?'

True, Dukhi didn't look as though he could be

anything but a gardener; but I wasn't satisfied with his denials or with Ayah's attempts to still my tongue. Hadn't Dukhi sent the Rani a nosegay?

When my father came home, he looked quite pleased with himself.

'What have you brought for me?' was the first question I asked.

He had brought me some new books, a dartboard, and a train set; and in my excitement over examining these gifts, I forgot to ask about the result of his trip.

It was during tiffin that he told me what had happened—and what was going to happen.

'We'll be going away soon,' he said. 'I've joined the Royal Air Force. I'll have to work in Delhi.'

'Oh! Will you be in the war, Dad? Will you fly a plane?'

'No, I'm too old to be flying planes. I'll be forty years in July. The RAF will be giving me what they call intelligence work—decoding secret messages and things like that and I don't suppose I'll be able to tell you much about it.'

This didn't sound as exciting as flying planes, but it sounded important and rather mysterious.

'Well, I hope it's interesting,' I said. 'Is Delhi a good place to live in?'

'I'm not sure. It will be very hot by the middle of April. And you won't be able to stay with me, Rusty— not at first, anyway, not until I can get family quarters . . . Meanwhile, you'll stay with your grandmother in Dehra.' He must have seen the disappointment in my face, because he quickly added, 'Of course I'll come to see you often. Dehra isn't far from Delhi—only a night's train journey.'

But I was dismayed. It wasn't that I didn't want to stay with my grandmother, but I had now grown so used to sharing my father's life and even watching him at work, that the thought of being separated from him was unbearable.

'Well, don't worry so much, Rusty, you will like being with your grandmother once again. She's very fond of you—ever since Grandfather passed away she has been more or less lonely. And if you come with me to Delhi, you'll be alone all day in a stuffy little hut while I'm away at work. Sometimes I may have to go on tour—then what happens?'

'I don't mind being on my own.' And this was true. Since my days in Java with Father I had already grown accustomed to having my own room and my own trunk and my own bookshelf and I now felt as though I was about to lose these things.

'Will Ayah come too?' I asked.

My father looked thoughtful. 'Would you like that?'

'Ayah must come,' I said firmly. 'Otherwise, I'll run away.'

'I'll have to ask her,' said my father.

Ayah, it turned out, was quite ready to come with us. In fact, she was indignant that Father should have considered leaving her behind. She was pleased and excited at the prospect of the move, and this helped to raise my spirits.

'Are there any books?' I asked my father. Books hadn't featured as an important part of my life the last time I was at my grandparents' house at Dehra. After all, that was when I was seven, and it was only recently— under my father's influence that I discovered the joys of reading and owning books.

'Your grandmother's books won't interest you. But I'll be bringing you books from Delhi whenever I come to see you.'

I was beginning to look forward to the move. A few days before we left, I went to say goodbye to the Rani.

'I'm going away,' I said.

'How lovely!' said the Rani. 'I wish I could go away!'

'Why don't you?'

'They won't let me. They're afraid to let me out of the palace.'

'What are they afraid of, Your Highness?'

'That I might run away. Run away, far far away, to the land where the leopards are learning to prey.'

Gosh, I thought, she's really quite crazy . . . But then she was silent, and started smoking a small hookah.

She drew on the hookah, looked at me, and asked, 'Where is your mother?'

'I haven't one.'

'Everyone has a mother. Did yours die?'

'No. She went away.'

She drew on her hookah again and then said, very sweetly, 'Don't go away . . .'

'I must,' I said. 'It's because of the war.'

'What war? Is there a war on? You see, no one tells me anything.'

'It's between us and Hitler,' I said.

'And who is Hitler?'

'He's a German.'

'I knew a German once, Dr Schreinherr, he had beautiful hands.'

'Was he an artist?'

'He was a dentist.'

The Rani got up from her couch and accompanied

me out on to the balcony. When we looked down at the garden, we could see Dukhi weeding a flower bed. Both of us gazed down at him in silence, and I wondered what the Rani would say if I asked her if she had ever been in love with the palace gardener. Ayah had told me it would be an insulting question, so I held my peace. But as I walked slowly down the spiral staircase, the Rani's voice came after me.

'Thank him,' she said. 'Thank him for the beautiful rose.'

The Last Tonga Ride

IT WAS A warm spring day in Dehra, and the walls of the bungalow were aflame with flowering bougainvillaea. The papayas were ripening. The scent of sweet peas drifted across the garden. Grandmother sat in an easy chair in a shady corner of the veranda, her knitting needles clicking away, her head nodding now and then. She was knitting a pullover for my father. 'Delhi has cold winters,' she had said, and although the winter was still eight months away, she had set to work on getting our woollens ready.

In the Kathiawar states, touched by the warm waters of the Arabian Sea, it had never been cold. But Dehra lies at the foot of the first range of the Himalayas.

Grandmother's hair was white and her eyes were not very strong, but her fingers moved quickly with the needles and the needles kept clicking all morning.

When Grandmother wasn't looking, I picked

geranium leaves, crushed them between my fingers and pressed them to my nose.

I had been in Dehra with Grandmother for almost a month and I had not seen my father during this time. He wrote to me every week, and sent me books and picture postcards, and I would walk to the end of the road to meet the postman as early as possible to see if there was any mail for us.

We heard the jingle of tonga bells at the gate and a familiar horse-buggy came rattling up the drive.

'I'll see who's come,' I said, and ran down the veranda steps and across the garden.

It was Bansi Lal in his tonga. There were many tongas and tonga-drivers in Dehra but Bansi was my favourite driver. He was young and handsome and always wore a clean white shirt and pyjamas. His pony, too, was bigger and faster than the other tonga ponies.

Bansi didn't have a passenger, so I asked him, 'What have you come for, Bansi?'

'Your grandmother sent for me, dost.' He did not call me 'chhota sahib' or 'baba', but 'dost' and this made me feel much more important. Not every small boy could boast of a tonga-driver for his friend!

'Where are you going, Granny?' I asked, after I had run back to the veranda.

'I'm going to the bank.'

'Can I come too?'

'Whatever for? What will you do in the bank?'

'Oh, I won't come inside, I'll sit in the tonga with Bansi.'

'Come along, then.'

We helped Grandmother into the back seat of the tonga, and then I joined Bansi in the driver's seat. He said something to his pony and the pony set off at a brisk trot, out of the gate and down the road.

'Now, not too fast, Bansi,' said Grandmother, who didn't like anything that went too fast—tonga, motor car, train or bullock cart.

'Fast?' said Bansi. 'Have no fear, memsahib. This pony has never gone fast in its life. Even if a bomb went off behind us, we could go no faster. I have another pony which I use for racing when customers are in a hurry. This pony is reserved for you, memsahib.'

There was no other pony, but Grandmother did not know this, and was mollified by the assurance that she was riding in the slowest tonga in Dehra.

A ten-minute ride brought us to the bazaar. Grandmother's bank, the Allahabad Bank, stood near the clock tower. She was gone for about half an hour and, during this period, Bansi and I sauntered about in front of the shops. The pony had been left with some green stuff to munch.

'Do you have any money on you?' asked Bansi.

'Four annas,' I said.

'Just enough for two cups of tea,' said Bansi, putting his arm round my shoulders and guiding me towards a tea stall. The money passed from my palm to his.

'You can have tea, if you like,' I said. 'I'll have a lemonade.'

'So be it, friend. A tea and a lemonade, and be quick about it,' said Bansi to the boy in the tea shop and presently the drinks were set before us and Bansi was making a sound rather like his pony when it drank, while I burped my way through some green, gaseous stuff that tasted more like soap than lemonade.

When Grandmother came out of the bank, she looked pensive and did not talk much during the ride back to the house except to tell me to behave myself when I leant over to pat the pony on its rump. After paying off Bansi, she marched straight indoors.

'When will you come again?' I asked Bansi.

'When my services are required, dost. I have to make a living, you know. But I tell you what, since we are friends, the next time I am passing this way after leaving a fare, I will jingle my bells at the gate and if you are free and would like a ride—a fast ride!—you can join me. It won't cost you anything. Just bring some money for a cup of tea.'

'All right—since we are friends,' I said.

'Since we are friends.'

And touching the pony very lightly with the handle of his whip, he sent the tonga rattling up the drive and out of the gate. I could hear Bansi singing as the pony cantered down the road.

Ayah was waiting for me in the bedroom, her hands resting on her broad hips—a sure sign of an approaching storm.

'So you went off to the bazaar without telling me,' she said. (It wasn't enough that I had Grandmother's permission!) 'And all this time I've been waiting to give you your bath.'

'It's too late now, isn't it?' I asked hopefully.

'No, it isn't. There's still an hour left for lunch. Off with your clothes!'

While I undressed, Ayah berated me for keeping the company of tonga-drivers like Bansi. I think she was a little jealous.

'He is a rogue, that man. He drinks, gambles, and smokes opium. He has T.B. and other terrible diseases. So don't you be too friendly with him, understand, baba?'

I nodded my head sagely but said nothing. I thought Ayah was exaggerating as she always did about people and, besides, I had no intention of giving up free tonga rides.

Dehra was a good place for trees, and Grandmother's house was surrounded by several kinds which I had not seen on my visit two years back, but all my favourite old trees were still there—the peepul, neem, mango, jackfruit, papaya and the ancient banyan tree. Some of these trees had been planted by my grandfather.

Blessed is the house upon whose walls the shade of an old tree softly falls.

I remember those lines of Granny's. They were true words, because it was a good house to live in.

'How old is the jackfruit tree?' I asked Grandmother.

'Now let me see,' said Grandmother, looking very thoughtful. 'I should remember the jackfruit tree. Oh yes, your grandfather put it down in 1911. It was during the rainy season. I remember because it was your father's birthday and we celebrated it by planting a tree—14 July 1911. Long before you were born!'

The banyan was an enormous tree, about sixty feet high, and I remember when I had first seen it I had been trembling with excitement because I had never seen such a marvellous tree before. I had approached it slowly, even cautiously, as I wasn't sure the tree wanted my friendship. It looked as though it had many secrets.

There were sounds and movements in the branches but I couldn't see who or what made the sounds.

The tree made the first move, the first overture of friendship. It allowed a leaf to fall.

The leaf brushed against my face as it floated down, but before it could reach the ground, I caught and held it. I studied the leaf, running my fingers over its smooth, glossy texture. Then I put out my hand and touched the rough bark of the tree and this felt good to me. So I removed my shoes and socks as people do when they enter a holy place, and finding first a foothold and then a handhold on that broad trunk, I pulled myself up with the help of the tree's aerial roots.

As I climbed, it seemed to me then that someone was helping me. Invisible hands, the hands of the spirit in the tree, touched me, and helped me climb.

But although the tree had wanted me, there were others who were disturbed and alarmed by my arrival. A pair of parrots suddenly shot out of a hole in the trunk and with shrill cries, flew across the garden— flashes of green and red and gold. A squirrel looked out from behind a branch, saw me, and went scurrying away to inform his friends and relatives. I hadn't wanted to cause any more commotion amongst all the birds and insects, so I made my way down the tree, happy to have made friends with the wonderful banyan in the first place.

Now, as if to renew that old friendship, I climbed the tree once again. I climbed high, looked up, and saw a red beak poised above my head. I shrank away, but the hornbill made no attempt to attack me. He was relaxing in his home, which was a great hole in the tree trunk.

Only the bird's head and great beak were showing. He looked at me in a rather bored way, drowsily opening and shutting his eyes. Suddenly he lunged at a passing cricket. Bill and tree trunk met with a loud and resonant 'Tonk!'

I was so startled that I nearly fell out of the tree. But it was a difficult tree to fall out of! It was full of places where one could sit or even lie down. I moved away from the hornbill, crawled along a branch which had sent out supports, and so moved quite a distance from the main body of the tree. I left its cold, dark depths for an area penetrated by shafts of sunlight.

No one could see me. I lay flat on the broad branch hidden by a screen of leaves. People passed by on the road below. A sahib in a sun-helmet, his memsahib twirling a coloured silk sun-umbrella. Obviously, she did not want to get too brown and be mistaken for a country-born person. Behind them, a pram wheeled along by a nanny.

Then there were a number of Indians—some in white dhotis, some in western clothes, some in loincloths. Some with baskets on their heads. Others with coolies to carry their baskets for them.

A cloud of dust, the blare of a horn, and down the road, like an out-of-condition dragon, came the latest Morris touring car. Then cyclists. Then a man with a basket of papayas balanced on his head. Following him, a man with a performing monkey. The monkey reminded me of Toto and Tutu. This man rattled a little hand-drum, and children followed man and monkey along the road. They stopped in the shade of a mango tree on the other side of the road. The little red monkey wore a frilled dress and a baby's bonnet. It danced for the children, while the man sang and played his drum.

The clip-clop of a tonga pony, and Bansi's tonga came rattling down the road. I called down to him and he reined in with a shout of surprise, and looked up into the branches of the banyan tree.

'What are you doing up there?' he cried.

'Hiding from Grandmother,' I said.

'And when are you coming for that ride?'

'On Tuesday afternoon,' I said.

'Why not today?'

'Ayah won't let me. But she has Tuesdays off.'

129

Bansi spat red paan juice across the road. 'Your ayah is jealous,' he said.

'I know,' I said. 'Women are always jealous, aren't they? I suppose it's because she doesn't have a tonga.'

'It's because she doesn't have a tonga-driver,' said Bansi, grinning up at me. 'Never mind. I'll come on Tuesday—that's the day after tomorrow, isn't it?'

I nodded down to him, and then started backing along my branch, because I could hear Ayah calling in the distance. Bansi leant forward and smacked his pony across the rump, and the tonga shot forward.

'What were you doing up there?' asked Ayah a little later.

'I was watching a snake cross the road,' I lied. I knew she couldn't resist talking about snakes. There weren't as many in Dehra as there had been in Kathiawar and she was thrilled that I had seen one.

'Was it moving towards you or away from you?' she asked.

'It was going away.'

Ayah's face clouded over. 'That means poverty for the beholder,' she said gloomily.

Later, while scrubbing me down in the bathroom, she began to air all her prejudices, which included drunkards ('they die quickly, anyway'), misers ('they get murdered sooner or later') and tonga-drivers ('they have all the vices').

'You are a very lucky boy,' she said suddenly, peering closely at my tummy.

'Why?' I asked. 'You just said I would be poor because I saw a snake going the wrong way.'

'Well, you won't be poor for long. You have a mole on your tummy and that's very lucky. And there is one under your armpit, which means you will be famous. Do you have one on the neck? No, thank God! A mole on the neck is the sign of a murderer!'

'Do you have any moles?' I asked.

Ayah nodded seriously, and pulling her sleeve up to her shoulder, showed me a large mole high on her arm.

'What does that mean?' I asked.

'It means a life of great sadness,' said Ayah miserably.

'Can I touch it?' I asked.

'Yes, touch it,' she said, and taking my hand, she placed it against the mole.

'It's a nice mole,' I said, wanting to make Ayah happy. 'Can I kiss it?'

'You can kiss it,' said Ayah.

I kissed her on the mole.

'That's nice,' she said.

Tuesday afternoon came at last, and as soon as Grandmother was asleep and Ayah had gone to the bazaar, I was at the gate, looking up and down the road for Bansi and his tonga. He was not long in coming. Before the tonga turned into the road, I could hear his voice, singing to the accompaniment of the carriage bells.

He reached down, took my hand, and hoisted me on to the seat beside him. Then we went off down the road at a steady jogtrot. It was only when we reached the outskirts of the town that Bansi encouraged his pony to greater efforts. He rose in his seat, leaned forward and slapped the pony across the haunches. From a brisk trot we changed to a carefree canter. The tonga swayed from side to side. I clung to Bansi's free arm, while he grinned at me, his mouth red with paan juice.

'Where shall we go, dost?' he asked.

'Nowhere,' I said. 'Anywhere.'

'We'll go to the river,' said Bansi.

The 'river' was really a swift mountain stream that ran through the forests outside Dehra, joining the Ganga about fifteen miles away. It was almost dry during the winter and early summer, in flood during the monsoon.

The road out of Dehra was a gentle decline and

132

soon we were rushing headlong through the tea gardens and eucalyptus forests, the pony's hooves striking sparks off the metalled road, the carriage wheels groaning and creaking so loudly that I feared one of them would come off and that we would all be thrown into a ditch or into the small canal that ran beside the road. We swept through mango groves, through guava and litchi orchards, past broadleaved sal and shisham trees. Once in the sal forest, Bansi turned the tonga on to a rough cart track, and we continued along it for about a furlong, until the road dipped down to the stream bed.

'Let us go straight into the water,' said Bansi. 'You and I and the pony!' And he drove the tonga straight into the middle of the stream, where the water came up to the pony's knees.

'I am not a great one for baths,' said Bansi, 'but the pony needs one, and why should a horse smell sweeter than its owner?' saying which, he flung off his clothes and jumped into the water.

'Better than bathing under a tap!' he cried, slapping himself on the chest and thighs. 'Come down, dost, and join me!'

After some hesitation I joined him, but had some difficulty in keeping on my feet in the fast current. I grabbed at the pony's tail and hung on to it, while

Bansi began sloshing water over the patient animal's back.

After this, Bansi led both me and the pony out of the stream and together we gave the carriage a good washing down. I'd had a free ride and Bansi got the services of a free helper for the long overdue spring-cleaning of his tonga. After we had finished the job, he presented me with a packet of *aam papad*—a sticky toffee made from mango pulp—and for some time I tore at it as a dog tears at a bit of old leather. Then I felt drowsy and lay down on the brown, sun-warmed grass. Crickets and grasshoppers were telephoning each other from tree and bush and a pair of blue jays rolled, dived, and swooped acrobatically overhead.

Bansi had no watch. He looked at the sun and said, 'It is past three. When will that ayah of yours be home? She is more frightening than your grandmother!'

'She comes at four.'

'Then we must hurry back. And don't tell her where we've been, or I'll never be able to come to your house again. Your grandmother's one of my best customers.'

'That means you'd be sorry if she died.'

'I would indeed, my friend.'

Bansi raced the tonga back to town. There was very little motor traffic in those days, and tongas and bullock carts were far more numerous than they are today.

We were back five minutes before Ayah returned. Before Bansi left, he promised to take me for another ride the following week. So for several weeks after this I went on free tonga rides with my friend, always wary that I'd be found out each time by Ayah. I was certain that if this were to happen, I would be on my last fun-filled tonga ride. Luckily for me though, she never caught me out.

Life with Uncle Ken

Granny's fabulous kitchen

As kitchens went, it wasn't all that big. It wasn't as big as the bedroom or the living room, but it was big enough, and there was a pantry next to it. What made it fabulous was all that came out of it: good things to eat like cakes and curries, chocolate fudge and peanut toffee, jellies and jam tarts, meat pies, stuffed turkeys, stuffed chickens, stuffed eggplants, and hams stuffed with stuffed chickens.

As far as I was concerned, Granny was the best cook in the whole wide world. If Granny was the best cook in the world, I must have been the boy with the best appetite.

Every winter, when I had a vacation from boarding school (my father had put me in a boarding school in Simla by now), I would spend about a month with Granny before going on to spend the rest of the holidays with my father in Delhi. Though Father was a reasonably good cook, he didn't have much time for it these days, so he employed a *khansama*—a professional cook—who made a good mutton curry but little else. Mutton curry for lunch and mutton curry for dinner could be a bit tiring, specially for a boy who liked to eat almost everything.

Granny was glad to have me because she lived alone most of the time. Not entirely alone, though . . . There was a gardener, Puran, who lived in an outhouse. And he had a son called Mohan, who was about my age. And there was Ayah, who had been with me for quite some time. She now lived with Granny—to keep her company and to help with the household work. And there was a Siamese cat with bright blue eyes, and a mongrel dog called Crazy because he ran circles round the house.

And, of course, there was Uncle Ken who came to stay whenever he was out of a job (which was quite often) or when he felt like enjoying some of Granny's cooking.

So Granny wasn't really alone. All the same, she was glad to have me. She didn't enjoy cooking for herself, she said; she had to cook for *someone*. And although the cat and the dog and sometimes Uncle Ken appreciated her efforts, a good cook likes to have a boy to feed, because boys are adventurous and ready to try the most unusual dishes.

Whenever Granny tried out a new recipe on me, she would wait for my comments and reactions, and then make a note in one of her exercise books. These notes were useful when she made the dish again, or when she tried it out on others.

'Do you like it?' she'd ask, after I'd taken a few mouthfuls.

'Yes, Gran.'

'Sweet enough?'

'Yes, Gran.'

'Not *too* sweet?'

'No, Gran.'

'Would you like some more?'

'Yes, please, Gran.'

'Well, finish it off.'

'If you say so, Gran.'

Roast Duck. This was one of Granny's specials. The first time I had roast duck at Granny's place, Uncle Ken was there too.

He'd just lost a job as a railway guard, and had come to stay with Granny until he could find another job. He always stayed as long as he could, only moving on when Granny offered to get him a job as an assistant master in Padre Lal's Academy for Small Boys. Uncle

Ken couldn't stand small boys. They made him nervous, he said. I made him nervous too, but there was only one of me, and there was always Granny to protect him. At Padre Lal's, there were over a hundred small boys.

Although Uncle Ken had a tremendous appetite, and ate just as much as I did, he never praised Granny's dishes. I think this was why I was annoyed with him at times, and why sometimes I enjoyed making him feel nervous.

Uncle Ken looked down at the roast duck, his glasses slipping down to the edge of his nose.

'Hm . . . Duck again, Aunt Ellen?'

'What do you mean, duck again? You haven't had duck since you were here last month.'

'That's what I mean,' said Uncle Ken. 'Somehow, one expects more variety from you, Aunt.'

All the same, he took two large helpings and ate most of the stuffing before I could get at it. I took my revenge by emptying all the apple sauce on to my plate. Uncle Ken knew I loved the stuffing; and I knew he was crazy about Granny's apple sauce. So we were even.

'When are you joining your father?' he asked hopefully, over the jam tart.

'I may not go to Delhi this year,' I said. 'When are you getting another job, Uncle?'

'Oh, I'm thinking of taking a rest for a couple of months.'

I enjoyed helping Granny and Ayah with the washing up. While we were at work, Uncle Ken would take a siesta on the veranda or switch on the radio to listen to dance music. Glenn Miller and his Swing Band was all the rage then.

'And how do you like your Uncle Ken?' asked Granny one day, as she emptied the bones from his plate into the dog's bowl.

'I wish he was someone else's uncle,' I said.

'He's not so bad, really. Just eccentric.'

'What's eccentric?'

'Oh, just a little crazy.'

'At least Crazy runs round the house,' I said. 'I've never seen Uncle Ken running.'

But I did one day.

Mohan and I were playing marbles in the shade of the mango grove when we were taken aback by the sight of Uncle Ken charging across the compound, pursued by a swarm of bees. He'd been smoking a cigar under a silk-cotton tree, and the fumes had disturbed the wild bees in their hive, directly above him. Uncle Ken fled indoors and leapt into a tub of cold water. He had received a few stings and decided to remain in bed for three days. Ayah took his meals to him on a tray.

'I didn't know Uncle Ken could run so fast,' I said, later that day.

'It's nature's way of compensating,' said Granny.

'What's compensating?'

'Making up for things . . . Now at least Uncle Ken knows that he can run. Isn't that wonderful?'

Whenever Granny made vanilla or chocolate fudge, she gave me some to take to Mohan. It was no use taking him roast duck or curried chicken because in his house no one ate meat. But Mohan liked sweets—Indian sweets, which were made with lots of milk and lots of sugar, as well as Granny's home-made English sweets.

We would climb into the branches of the jackfruit tree and eat fudge or peppermints or sticky toffee. We couldn't eat the jackfruit, except when it was cooked as a vegetable or made into a pickle. But the tree itself was wonderful for climbing. And some wonderful creatures lived in it—squirrels and fruit bats and a pair of green parrots. The squirrels were friendly and soon got into the habit of eating from our hands. They, too, were fond of chocolate fudge. One young squirrel would even explore my pockets to see if I was keeping anything from him.

Mohan and I could climb almost any tree in the garden, and if Granny was looking for us, she'd call from the front veranda and then from the back veranda and then from the pantry at the side of the house and, finally, from her bathroom window on the other side of the house. There were trees on all sides and it was impossible to tell which one we were in, until we answered her call. Sometimes Crazy would give us away by barking beneath our tree.

When there was fruit to be picked, Mohan did the picking. The mangoes and litchis came into season during the summer, when I was away at boarding school, so I couldn't help with the fruit gathering. The papayas were in season during the winter, but you don't climb papaya trees, they are too slender and wobbly. You knock the papayas down with a long pole.

Mohan also helped Granny with the pickling. She was justly famous for her pickles. Green mangoes pickled in oil were always popular. So was her hot lime pickle. And she was equally good at pickling turnips, carrots, cauliflowers, chillies, and other fruits and vegetables. She could pickle almost anything, from a nasturtium seed to a jackfruit. Uncle Ken didn't care for pickles, so I was always urging Granny to make more of them.

My own preference was for sweet chutneys and sauces, but I ate pickles too, even the very hot ones.

One winter, when Granny's funds were low,

Mohan and I went from house to house, selling pickles for her.

In spite of all the people and pets she fed, Granny wasn't rich. The house had come to her from Grandfather, but there wasn't much money in the bank. The mango crop brought in a fair amount every year, and there was a small pension from the Forest Service but there was no other income. And now that I come to think of it, all those wonderful meals consisted only of one course, followed by a sweet dish. It was Granny's cooking that turned a modest meal into a feast.

I wasn't ashamed to sell pickles for Granny. It was great fun. Mohan and I armed ourselves with baskets filled with pickle bottles, then set off to cover all the houses in our area.

Major Wilkie, across the road, was our first customer. He had a red beard and bright blue eyes and was almost always good-humoured.

'And what have you got there, young Bond?' he asked.

'Pickles, sir.'

'Pickles! Have you been making them?'

'No, sir, they're my grandmother's. We're selling them, so we can buy a turkey for Christmas.'

'Mrs Bond's pickles, eh? Well, I'm glad mine is the first house on your way, because I'm sure that basket will soon be empty. There is no one who can make a pickle like your grandmother, son. I've said it before and I'll say it again, she's God's gift to a world that's terribly short of good cooks. My wife's gone shopping, so I can talk quite freely, you see . . . What have you got this time? Stuffed chillies, I trust. She knows they're my favourite. I shall be deeply wounded if there are no stuffed chillies in that basket.'

There were, in fact, three bottles of stuffed red chillies in the basket, and Major Wilkie took all of them.

Our next call was at Miss Ridgewood's house. Miss Ridgewood couldn't eat hot food, so it was no use offering her pickles. But she bought a bottle of preserved ginger. And she gave me a little prayer book. Whenever I went to see her, she gave me a new prayer book. Soon, I had quite a collection of prayer books. What was I to do with them? Finally, Uncle Ken took them off me, and sold them to the Children's Academy.

Further down the road, Dr Dutt, who was in charge of the hospital, bought several bottles of lime pickles, saying it was good for his liver. And Mr Hari, who owned a garage at the end of the road and sold all the latest cars, bought two bottles of pickled onions and begged us to bring him another two the following month.

By the time we got home, the basket would usually be empty, and Granny richer by twenty or thirty rupees-enough, in those days, for a turkey.

'It's high time you found a job,' said Granny to Uncle Ken one day.

'There are no jobs in Dehra,' complained Uncle Ken.

'How can you tell? You've never looked for one. And anyway, you don't have to stay here for ever. Your sister Emily is headmistress of a school in Lucknow. You could go to her. She said she was ready to put you in charge of a dormitory.'

'Bah!' said Uncle Ken. 'Honestly, Aunt, you don't expect me to look after a dormitory seething with forty or fifty demented small boys?'

'What's demented?' I asked.

'Shut up,' said Uncle Ken.

'It means crazy,' said Granny.

'So many words mean crazy,' I complained. 'Why don't we just say crazy. We have a crazy dog, and now Uncle Ken is crazy too.'

Uncle Ken clipped me over my ear, and Granny said, 'Your uncle isn't crazy, so don't be disrespectful. He's just lazy.'

'And eccentric,' I said. 'I heard he was eccentric.'

'Who said I was eccentric?' demanded Uncle Ken.

'Miss Leslie,' I lied. I knew Uncle Ken was fond of Miss Leslie, who ran a beauty parlour in Dehra's smart shopping centre, Astley Hall.

'I don't believe you,' said Uncle Ken. 'Anyway, when did you see Miss Leslie?'

'We sold her a bottle of mint chutney last week. I told her you liked mint chutney. But she said she'd bought it for Mr Brown who's taking her to the pictures tomorrow.'

'Eat well, but don't overeat,' Granny used to tell me. 'Good food is a gift from God, and like any other gift, it can be misused.'

She'd made a list of kitchen proverbs and pinned it to the pantry door—not so high that I couldn't read it, either. These were some of the proverbs:

LIGHT SUPPERS MAKE LONG LIVES.

BETTER A SMALL FISH THAN AN EMPTY DISH.

THERE IS SKILL IN ALL THINGS, EVEN IN MAKING PORRIDGE.

EATING AND DRINKING SHOULD NOT KEEP MEN FROM THINKING.

DRY BREAD AT HOME IS BETTER THAN ROAST MEAT ABROAD.

A GOOD DINNER SHARPENS THE WIT AND SOFTENS THE HEART.

LET NOT YOUR TONGUE CUT YOUR THROAT.

Uncle Ken does nothing

To our surprise, Uncle Ken got a part-time job as a guide, showing tourists the 'sights' around Dehra.

There was an old fort near the river bed; and a seventeenth-century temple; and a jail where Pandit Nehru had spent some time as a political prisoner; and, about ten miles into the foothills, the hot sulphur springs.

Uncle Ken told us he was taking a party of six American tourists, husbands and wives to the sulphur springs. Granny was pleased. Uncle Ken was busy at last! She gave him a hamper filled with ham sandwiches, home made biscuits and a dozen oranges—ample provision for a day's outing.

The sulphur springs were only ten miles from Dehra, but we didn't see Uncle Ken for three days.

He was a sight when he got back. His clothes were dusty and torn; his cheeks were sunken; and the little bald patch on top of his head had been burnt a bright red.

'What have you been doing to yourself?' asked Granny.

Uncle Ken sank into the armchair on the veranda. 'I'm starving, Aunt Ellen. Give me something to eat.'

'What happened to the food you took with you?'

'There were seven of us, and it was all finished on the first day.'

'Well it was only supposed to last a day. You said you were going to the sulphur springs.'

'Yes, that's where we were going,' said Uncle Ken. 'But we never reached them. We got lost in the hills.'

'How could you possibly have got lost in the hills? You had only to walk straight along the river bed and up the valley . . . *You* ought to know, you were the guide and you'd been there before, when my husband was alive.'

'Yes, I know,' said Uncle Ken, looking crestfallen. 'But I forgot the way. That is, I forgot the valley. I mean, I took them up the wrong valley. And I kept thinking the springs would be at the same river, but it wasn't the same river . . . So we kept walking, until we were in the hills, and then I looked down and saw we'd come up the wrong valley. We had to spend the night under the stars. It was very, very cold. And next day I thought we'd come back a quicker way through Mussoorie, but we took the wrong path and reached Kempti instead . . . And then we walked down to the motor road and caught a bus.'

I helped Granny put Uncle Ken to bed, and then helped her make him a strengthening onion soup. I took him the soup on a tray, and he made a face while drinking it and then asked for more. He was in bed for two days, while Ayah and I took turns taking him his meals. He wasn't a bit grateful.

When Uncle Ken complained he was losing his hair and that his bald patch was increasing in size, Granny looked up her book of old recipes and said there was one for baldness which Grandfather had used with great success. It consisted of a lotion made with gherkins soaked in brandy. Uncle Ken said he'd try it.

Granny soaked some gherkins in brandy for a week, then gave the bottle to Uncle Ken with instructions to rub a little into his scalp mornings and evenings.

Next day, when she looked into his room, she found only gherkins in the bottle. Uncle Ken had drunk all the brandy.

Uncle Ken liked to whistle.

Hands in his pockets, nothing to do, he would stroll about the house, around the garden, up and down the road, whistling feebly to himself.

It was always the same whistle, tuneless to everyone except my uncle.

'What are you whistling today, Uncle Ken?' I'd ask.

'*Ol' Man River*. Don't you recognize it?' And the next time around he'd be whistling the same notes, and I'd say, 'Still whistling *Ol' Man River*, Uncle?'

'No, I'm not. This is *Danny Boy*. Can't you tell the difference?'

And he'd slouch off, whistling tunelessly.

Sometimes it irritated Granny.

'Can't you stop whistling, Ken? It gets on my nerves. Why don't you try singing for a change?'

'I can't. It's *The Blue Danube*, there aren't any words,' and he'd waltz around the kitchen, whistling.

'Well, you can do your whistling and waltzing on the veranda,' Granny would say. 'I won't have it in the kitchen. It spoils the food.'

When Uncle Ken had a bad tooth removed by our dentist, Dr Kapadia, we thought his whistling would stop. But it only became louder and shriller.

One day, while he was strolling along the road, hands in his pockets, doing nothing, whistling very loudly, a girl on a bicycle passed him. She stopped suddenly, got off the bicycle, and blocked his way.

'If you whistle at me every time I pass, Kenneth Clerke,' she said, 'I'll wallop you!'

Uncle Ken went red in the face. 'I wasn't whistling at you,' he said.

'Well, I don't see anyone else on the road.'

'I was whistling *God Save The King*. Don't you recognize it?'

Uncle Ken on the job

'We'll have to do something about Uncle Ken,' said Granny to the world at large.

I was in the kitchen with her, shelling peas and popping a few into my mouth now and then. Suzie, the Siamese cat, sat on the sideboard, patiently watching Granny prepare an Irish stew. Suzie liked Irish stew.

'It's not that I mind him staying,' said Granny, 'and I don't want any money from him, either. But it isn't healthy for a young man to remain idle for so long.'

'Is Uncle Ken a young man, Gran?'

'He's forty. Everyone says he'll improve as he grows up.'

'He could go and live with Aunt Mabel.'

'He *does* go and live with Aunt Mabel. He also lives with Aunt Emily and Aunt Beryl. That's his trouble—he has too many doting sisters ready to put him up and put up with him . . . Their husbands are all quite well-off and can afford to have him now and then. So our Ken spends three months with Mabel, three months with Beryl, three months with me. That way he gets through the year as everyone's guest and doesn't have to worry about making a living.'

'He's lucky in a way,' I said.

'His luck won't last for ever. Already Mabel is talking of going to New Zealand. And once India is free—in just a few years from now—Emily and Beryl will probably go off to England, because their husbands are in the army and all the British officers will be leaving.'

'Can't Uncle Ken follow them to England?'

'He knows he'll have to start working if he goes there. When your aunts find they have to manage without servants, they won't be ready to keep Ken for long periods. In any case, who's going to pay his fare to England or New Zealand?'

'If he can't go, he'll stay here with you, Granny. You'll be here, won't you?'

'Not for ever. Only while I live.'

'You won't go to England?'

'No, I've grown up here. I'm like the trees. I've taken root, I won't be going away—not until, like an old tree, I'm without any more leaves . . . You'll go, though, when you are bigger. You'll probably finish your schooling abroad.'

'I'd rather finish it here. I want to spend all my holidays with you. If I go away, who'll look after you when you grow old?'

'I'm old already. Over sixty.'

'Is that very old? It's only a little older than Uncle Ken. And how will you look after him when you're *really* old?'

'He can look after himself if he tries. And it's time he started. It's time he took a job.'

I pondered on the problem. I could think of nothing that would suit Uncle Ken—or rather, I could think of no one who would find him suitable. It was Ayah who made a suggestion.

'The Maharani of Jetpur needs a tutor for her children,' she said. 'Just a boy and a girl.'

'How do you know?' asked Granny.

'I heard it from their ayah. The pay is two hundred rupees a month, and there is not much work—only two hours every morning.'

'That should suit Uncle Ken,' I said.

'Yes, it's a good idea,' said Granny. 'We'll have to talk him into applying. He ought to go over and see them. The Maharani is a good person to work for.'

Uncle Ken agreed to go over and inquire about the job. The Maharani was out when he called, but he was interviewed by the Maharaja.

'Do you play tennis?' asked the Maharaja.

'Yes,' said Uncle Ken, who remembered having played a bit of tennis when he was a schoolboy.

'In that case, the job's yours. I've been looking for

a fourth player for a doubles match . . . By the way, were you at Cambridge?'

'No, I was at Oxford,' said Uncle Ken.

The Maharaja was impressed. An Oxford man who could play tennis was just the sort of tutor he wanted for his children.

When Uncle Ken told Granny about the interview, she said, 'But you haven't been to Oxford, Ken. How could you say that!'

'Of course I have been to Oxford. Don't you remember? I spent two years there with your brother Jim!'

'Yes, but you were helping him in his pub in the town. You weren't at the University.'

'Well, the Maharaja never asked me if I had been to the University. He asked me if I was at Cambridge, and I said no, I was at Oxford, which was perfectly true. He didn't ask me what I was doing at Oxford. What difference does it make?' And he strolled off, whistling.

To our surprise, Uncle Ken was a great success in his job. In the beginning, anyway.

The Maharaja was such a poor tennis player that he was delighted to discover that there was someone who was even worse. So, instead of becoming a doubles partner for the Maharaja, Uncle Ken became his favourite singles opponent. As long as he could keep losing to His Highness, Uncle Ken's job was safe.

In between tennis matches and accompanying his employer on duck shoots, Uncle Ken squeezed in a few lessons for the children, teaching them reading, writing and arithmetic. Sometimes he took me along, so that I could tell him when he got his sums wrong. Uncle Ken wasn't very good at subtraction, although he could add fairly well.

The Maharaja's children were smaller than me. Uncle Ken would leave me with them, saying, 'Just see that they do their sums properly, Rusty,' and he would stroll off to the tennis courts, hands in his pockets, whistling tunelessly.

Even if his pupils had different answers to the same sum, he would give both of them an encouraging pat, saying, 'Excellent, excellent. I'm glad to see both of you trying so hard. One of you is right and one of you is wrong, but as I don't want to discourage either of you, I won't say who's right and who's wrong!'

But afterwards, on the way home, he'd ask me, 'Which was the right answer, Rusty?'

Uncle Ken always maintained that he would never have lost his job if he hadn't beaten the Maharaja at tennis.

Not that Uncle Ken had any intention of winning.

But by playing occasional games with the Maharaja's secretaries and guests, his tennis had improved and so, try as hard as he might to lose, he couldn't help winning a match against his employer.

The Maharaja was furious.

'Mr Clerke,' he said sternly, 'I don't think you realize the importance of losing. We can't all win, you know. Where would the world be without losers?'

'I'm terribly sorry,' said Uncle Ken. 'It was just a fluke, Your Highness.'

The Maharaja accepted Uncle Ken's apologies, but a week later it happened again. Kenneth Clerke won and the Maharaja stormed off the court without saying a word. The following day he turned up at lesson time. As usual Uncle Ken and the children were engaged in a game of noughts and crosses.

'We won't be requiring your services from tomorrow, Mr Clerke. I've asked my secretary to give you a month's salary in lieu of notice.'

Uncle Ken came home with his hands in his pockets, whistling cheerfully.

'You're early,' said Granny.

'They don't need me any more,' said Uncle Ken.

'Oh well, never mind. Come in and have your tea.'

Granny must have known the job wouldn't last very long. And she wasn't one to nag. As she said later, 'At least he tried. And it lasted longer than most of his jobs—two months.'

Uncle Ken at the wheel

On my next visit to Dehra, Mohan met me at the station. We got into a tonga with my luggage and we went rattling and jingling along Dehra's quiet roads to Granny's house.

'Tell me all the news, Mohan.'

'Not much to tell. Some of the sahibs are selling their houses and going away. Suzie has had kittens.'

Granny knew I'd been in the train for a day and a night and she had a huge breakfast ready for me. Porridge, scrambled eggs on toast. Bacon with fried tomatoes. Toast and marmalade. Sweet milky tea.

She told me there'd been a letter from Uncle Ken.

'He says he's the assistant manager of Firpo's hotel in Simla,' she said. 'The salary is very good, and he gets free board and lodging. It's a steady job and I hope he keeps it.'

Three days later Uncle Ken was on the veranda steps with his bedding roll and battered suitcase.

'Have you given up the hotel job?' asked Granny.

'No,' said Uncle Ken. 'They have closed down.'

'I hope it wasn't because of you.'

'No, Aunt Ellen. The bigger hotels in the hill stations are all closing down.'

'Well, never mind. Come along and have your tiffin. There is a kofta curry today. It's Rusty's favourite.'

'Oh, is he here too? I have far too many nephews and nieces. Still he's preferable to those two girls of Mabel's. They made life miserable for me all the time I was with them in Simla.'

Over tiffin, Uncle Ken talked very seriously about ways and means of earning a living. 'There is only one taxi in the whole of Dehra,' he mused. 'Surely there is business for another?'

'I'm sure there is,' said Granny. 'But where does it get you? In the first place, you don't have a taxi. And in the second place, you can't drive.'

'I can soon learn. There's a driving school in town. And I can use Uncle Bond's old car. It's been gathering dust in the garage for years.' (He was referring to Grandfather's vintage Hillman Roadster. It was a 1926 model: about fifteen years old.)

'I don't think it will run now,' said Granny.

'Of course it will. It just needs some oiling and greasing and a spot of paint.'

'All right, learn to drive. Then we will see about the Roadster.'

So Uncle Ken joined the driving school.

He was very regular, going for his lessons for an hour in the evening. Granny paid the fee.

After a month, Uncle Ken announced that he could drive and that he was taking the Roadster out for a trial run.

'You haven't got your licence yet,' said Granny.

'Oh, I won't take her far,' said Uncle Ken. 'Just down the road and back again.'

He spent all morning cleaning up the car. Granny gave him money for a can of petrol.

After tea, Uncle Ken said, 'Come along, Rusty, hop in and I will give you a ride. Bring Mohan along too.'

Mohan and I needed no urging. We got into the car beside Uncle Ken.

'Now don't go too fast, Ken,' said Granny anxiously. 'You are not used to the car as yet.'

Uncle Ken nodded and smiled and gave two sharp toots on the horn. He was feeling pleased with himself.

Driving through the gate, he nearly ran over Crazy.

Miss Ridgewood, coming out for her evening rickshaw ride, saw Uncle Ken at the wheel of the Roadster and went indoors again.

Uncle Ken drove straight and fast, tootling the horn without a break.

At the end of the road there was a roundabout.

'We'll turn here,' said Uncle Ken, 'and then drive back again.'

He turned the steering wheel; we began going round the roundabout; but the steering wheel wouldn't turn all the way, not as much as Uncle Ken would have liked it to . . . So, instead of going round, we took a right turn and kept going, straight on—and straight through the Maharaja of Jetpur's garden wall.

It was a single-brick wall, and the Roadster knocked it down and emerged on the other side without any damage to the car or any of its occupants. Uncle Ken brought it to a halt in the middle of the Maharaja's lawn.

Running across the grass came the Maharaja himself, flanked by his secretaries and their assistants.

When he saw that it was Uncle Ken at the wheel, the Maharaja beamed with pleasure.

'Delighted to see you, old chap!' he exclaimed. 'Jolly decent of you to drop in again. How about a game of tennis?'

Uncle Ken at the wicket

Although restored to the Maharaja's favour, Uncle Ken was still without a job.

Granny refused to let him take the Hillman out again and so he decided to sulk. He said it was all Grandfather's fault for not seeing to the steering wheel while he was still alive. Uncle Ken went on a hunger strike for two hours (between tiffin and tea), and we did not hear him whistle for several days.

'The blessedness of silence,' said Granny.

And then he announced that he was going to Lucknow to stay with Aunt Emily.

'She has three children and a school to look after,' said Granny. 'Don't stay too long.'

'She doesn't mind how long I stay,' said Uncle Ken and off he went.

His visit to Lucknow was a memorable one, and we only heard about it much later.

When Uncle Ken got down at Lucknow station, he found himself surrounded by a large crowd, everyone waving to him and shouting words of welcome in Hindi, Urdu and English. Before he could make out what it was all about, he was smothered by garlands of marigolds. A young man came forward and announced, 'The Gomti Cricketing Association welcomes you to the historical city of Lucknow,' and promptly led Uncle Ken out of the station to a waiting car.

It was only when the car drove into the sports stadium that Uncle Ken realized that he was expected to play in a cricket match.

This is what had happened.

Bruce Hallam, the famous English cricketer, was touring India and had agreed to play in a charity match at Lucknow. But the previous evening, in Delhi, Bruce had gone to bed with an upset stomach and hadn't been able to get up in time to catch the train. A telegram was sent to the organizers of the match in Lucknow; but, like many a telegram, it did not reach its destination. The cricket fans of Lucknow had arrived at the station in droves to welcome the great cricketer. And by a strange coincidence, Uncle Ken bore a startling resemblance to Bruce Hallam; even the bald patch on the crown of his head was exactly like Hallam's. Hence the muddle. And, of course, Uncle Ken was always happy to enter into the spirit of a muddle.

Having received from the Gomti Cricketing Association a rousing reception and a magnificent breakfast at the stadium, he felt that it would be very unsporting on his part if he refused to play cricket for them. 'If I can hit a tennis ball,' he mused, 'I ought to be able to hit a cricket ball.' And luckily there was a blazer and a pair of white flannels in his suitcase.

The Gomti team won the toss and decided to bat. Uncle Ken was expected to go in at number three, Bruce Hallam's usual position. And he soon found himself walking to the wicket, wondering why on earth no one had as yet invented a more comfortable kind of pad.

The first ball he received was short-pitched, and he was able to deal with it in tennis fashion, swatting it to the mid-wicket boundary. He got no runs, but the crowd cheered.

The next ball took Uncle Ken on the pad. He was right in front of his wicket and should have been given out lbw. But the umpire hesitated to raise his finger. After all, hundreds of people had paid good money to see Bruce Hallam play, and it would have been a shame to disappoint them. 'Not out,' said the umpire.

The third ball took the edge of Uncle Ken's bat and sped through the slips.

'Lovely shot!' exclaimed an elderly gentleman in the pavilion.

'A classic late cut,' said another.

The ball reached the boundary and Uncle Ken had four runs to his name. Then it was 'Over', and the other batsman had to face the bowling. He took a run off the first ball and called for a second run. Uncle Ken thought one run was more than enough. Why go charging up and down the wicket like a mad man? However, he couldn't refuse to run, and he was halfway down the pitch when the fielder's throw hit the wicket. Uncle Ken was run-out by yards. There could be no doubt about it this time.

He returned to the pavilion to the sympathetic applause of the crowd.

'Not his fault,' said the elderly gentleman. 'The other chap shouldn't have called. There wasn't a run there. Still, it was worth coming here all the way from Kanpur if only to see that superb late cut . . .'

Uncle Ken enjoyed a hearty tiffin-lunch (taken at noon), and then, realizing that the Gomti team would probably have to be in the field for most of the afternoon—more running about!—he slipped out of the pavilion, left the stadium, and took a tonga to Aunt Emily's house in the cantonment.

He was just in time for a second lunch (taken at one o'clock) with Aunt Emily's family: and it was presumed at the stadium that Bruce Hallam had left early to catch the train to Allahabad, where he was expected to play in another charity match.

Aunt Emily, a forceful woman, fed Uncle Ken for a week, and then put him to work in the boys' dormitory of her school. It was several months before he was able to save up enough money to run away and return to Granny's place.

But he had the satisfaction of knowing that he had helped the great Bruce Hallam add another four runs to his grand aggregate. The scorebook of the Gomti Cricketing Association had recorded his feat for all time:

'B. Hallam run-out: 4.'

The Gomti team lost the match. But, as Uncle Ken would readily admit, where would we be without losers?

The Ghost in the Garden

BEHIND THE HOUSE there was an orchard where guava, litchi and papaya trees mingled with two or three tall mango trees. The guava trees were easy to climb. The litchi trees gave a lot of shade—as well as bunches of delicious lichees in the summer. The mango trees were at their most attractive in the spring, when their blossoms gave out a heady fragrance.

But there was one old mango tree, near the boundary wall, where no one, not even Puran, our gardener, ever went.

'It doesn't give any fruit,' said Puran, when I questioned him. 'It's an old tree.'

'Then why don't we cut it down?'

'We will, one day, when your grandmother wishes . . .'

The weeds grew thick in that corner of the garden. They were safe there from Puran's relentless weeding.

'Why doesn't anyone go to that corner of the

orchard?' I asked Miss Kellner, our crippled tenant, who had been in Dehra since she was a girl.

But she didn't want to talk about it. Uncle Ken, too, changed the subject whenever I brought it up.

So I wandered about the orchard on my own, cautiously making my way towards that neglected and forbidden corner of the garden until Puran called me back.

'Don't go there, baba,' he cautioned. 'It's unlucky.'

'Why doesn't anyone go near the old mango tree?' I asked Granny.

She just shook her head and turned away. There was obviously something that no one wanted me to know. So I disobeyed and ignored everyone, and in the still of the afternoon, when most of the household was taking a siesta, I walked over to the old mango tree at the end of the garden.

It was a cool, shady place, and seemed friendly enough. But there were no birds in the tree, no squirrels, either. And this was unusual. I sat down on the grass, with my back against the trunk of the tree, and peered out at the sunlit house and garden. In the shimmering heat haze I thought I saw someone walking through the trees, but it wasn't Puran or anyone I knew.

It had been a hot day, but presently I began to feel

cold; and then I found myself shivering, as though a fever had suddenly come on. I looked up into the tree, and the branch above me was moving, swaying slightly, although there was no breeze and all the other leaves and branches were still.

I felt I had to get out of the cold, but I found it difficult to get up. So I crawled across the grass on my hands and knees, until I was in the bright sunlight. The shivering passed and I ran across to the house and did not look back at the mango tree until I had reached the veranda.

I told Miss Kellner about my experience.

'Were you frightened?' she asked.

'Yes—a little,' I confessed.

'And did you see anything?'

'Some of the branches moved—I felt very cold—but there was no wind.'

'Did you hear anything?'

'Just a soft moaning sound.'

'It's an old tree. It groans when it feels its age—just as I do!'

I did not go near the mango tree for some time, and I did not mention the incident to Granny or Uncle Ken. I had by now realized that the subject was taboo with them.

❖

As a boy I was always exploring lonely places—neglected gardens and orchards, unoccupied houses, patches of scrub or wasteland, the fields outside the town, the fringes of the forest. On one of my rambles behind the bungalow, I pushed my way through a thicket of lantana bushes and stumbled over a thick stone slab, twisting my ankle slightly as I fell. For some time I sat on the grass massaging my foot. When the pain eased, I looked more closely at the stone slab and was surprised to find that it was a gravestone. It was almost entirely covered by ivy; obviously no one had been near it for years. I tugged at the ivy and some of it came away in my hands. There was some indistinct lettering on the grave, half-obscured by grass and moss. I could make out a name—Rose—but little more.

I sat there for some time, pondering over my discovery, and wondering why 'Rose' should have been buried at so lonely a spot when there was a cemetery not far away. Why hadn't she been interred beside her kith and kin? Had she wished it so? And why?

Only Miss Kellner seemed willing to answer my questions, and it was to her I went, where she sat in her armchair under the pomalo tree—the armchair from which she never moved except when she was carried bodily to her bed or bathroom by the ayah or a couple of her rickshaw boys. I can never forget

crippled Miss Kellner in her armchair in the garden, playing patience with a well-worn pack of cards—and always patient with me whenever I interrupted her game with endless questions about neighbours or relatives or her own history. Even as a boy, the past fascinated me. I don't mean the history of nations; I mean individual histories, the way people lived, and why they were happy or unhappy, and why they sometimes did terrible things for no apparent rhyme or reason.

'Miss Kellner,' I asked, 'whose grave is that in the jungle behind the house?'

She looked at me over the rim of her pince-nez. 'How would you expect me to know, child? Do I look as though I could climb walls, looking for old graves? Have you asked your grandmother?'

'Granny won't tell me anything. And Uncle Ken pretends to know everything when he knows nothing.'

'So how should I know?'

'You've been here a long time.'

'Only twenty years. That happened before I came to this house.'

'*What* happened?'

'Oh, you are a trying boy. Why must you know everything?'

'It's better than *not* knowing.'

'Are you sure? Sometimes it's better not to know.'

'Sometimes, maybe . . . But I *like* to know. Who was Rose?'

'Your grandfather's first wife.'

'Oh.' This came as a surprise. I hadn't heard about Grandfather's first marriage. 'But why is she buried in such a lonely place? Why not in the cemetery?'

'Because she took her own life. And in those days a suicide couldn't be given Christian burial in a cemetery. Now is your curiosity satisfied?'

But my appetite had only been whetted for more information. 'And why did she commit suicide?'

'I really don't know, child. Why would anyone? Because they are unhappy, tired of living, in distress over something or the other.'

'You're not tired of living, are you? Even though you can't walk and your fingers are all crooked . . .'

'Don't be rude, or you won't find any meringues in my pantry! My fingers are good enough for writing, and for poking small boys in the ribs.' And she gave me a sharp poke which made me yelp. 'No, I'm not tired of life—not yet—but people are made differently, you know. And your grandfather isn't around to tell us what happened. And of course he married again—your grandmother . . .'

'Would *she* have known the first one?'

'I don't think so. She met your grandfather much later. But she doesn't like to talk about these things.'

'And how did Rose commit suicide?'

'I have no idea.'

'Of course you know, Miss Kellner. You can't bluff me. You know everything!'

'I wasn't here, I tell you.'

'But you heard all about it. And I know how she did it. She must have hanged herself from that mango tree— the tree at the end of the garden, which everyone avoids. I told you I went there one day, and it was very cold and lonely in its shade. I was frightened, you know.'

'Yes,' said Miss Kellner pensively. 'She must have been lonely, poor thing. She wasn't very stable, I'm told. Used to wander about on her own, picking wildflowers, singing to herself, sometimes getting lost and coming home at odd hours. How does the old song go? "Lonely as the desert breeze . . ."' In her croaky voice, Miss Kellner sang a refrain from an old ballad, before continuing, 'Your grandfather was very fond of her. He wasn't a cruel man. He put up with her strange ways. But sometimes he lost patience and scolded her and once or twice had to even lock her up. *That* was frightening, because then she would start screaming. It was a mistake locking her up. Never lock anyone up,

174

child . . . Something seemed to snap inside her. She became violent at times.'

'How do you know all this, Miss Kellner?'

'Your grandfather would sometimes come over and tell me his troubles. I was living in another house then, a little way down the road. Poor man, he had a trying time with Rose. He was thinking of sending her to Ranchi, to the mental hospital. Then, early one morning, he found her hanging from the mango tree. Her spirit had flown away, like the bluebird she always wanted to be.'

After that, I did not go near the old mango tree; I found it rather menacing, as though it had actually participated in that dark deed . . . Poor innocent tree, being saddled with the emotions of unbalanced humans! But I visited the neglected grave and cleaned the weeds away, so that the inscription stood out more clearly: 'Rose, dearly beloved wife of Henry Bond'. And when Puran wasn't looking, I plucked a red rose from the garden and placed it on the grave.

One afternoon, when Granny was at a bridge party and Uncle Ken was taking a walk, I rummaged through the storeroom adjoining the back veranda, leafing through old scrapbooks and magazines. Behind a pile of books I discovered an old wind-up gramophone, an album of well-preserved gramophone records, and a box of steel needles. I took the gramophone into the sitting-room and tried out one of the records. It sounded all right. So I played a few more. They were all songs of yesteryear, romantic ballads sung by tenors and baritones who were popular in the 1920s and 30s. Granny did not listen to music, and the gramophone had been neglected a long time. Now, for the first time in many years, the room was full of melody. *One Alone, I'll See You Again, Will You Remember? Only A Rose* . . .

Only a rose
to give you,
Only a song
dying away, Only a smile
to keep in memory

It was while this tender love song was playing that a transformation seemed to come over the room.

At first it grew darker. Then a soft pink glow suffused the room, and I saw the figure of a woman, a smiling melancholy woman in white, drifting, rather than walking, towards me. She stopped in the centre of the room, and appeared to be watching me. She wore the long flowing dress of an earlier day, and her hair was arranged in a sort of coiffure that I'd seen in old photographs.

As the song came to an end, the apparition vanished. The room was normal again. I put away the gramophone and the records. I felt disturbed rather than afraid, and I did not wish to conjure up further emanations from the past.

But in my dreams that night I saw the beautiful sad lady again. She was waltzing in the garden, sometimes by herself, sometimes partnered by other phantom dancers. She beckoned to me in my dream, inviting me to join her, but I remained standing on the veranda steps until she danced away into the distance and faded from view.

And in the morning when I woke I found a red rose, moist with dew, lying beside my pillow.

The Photograph

I WAS TEN years old. My grandmother sat on the string bed under the mango tree. It was late summer and there were sunflowers in the garden and a warm wind in the trees. My grandmother was knitting a woollen scarf for the winter months. She was very old, dressed in a plain white dress. Her eyes were not very strong now but her fingers moved quickly with the needles and the needles kept clicking all afternoon. Grandmother had white hair but there were very few wrinkles on her skin.

I was back in Dehra for my vacations from boarding school. Now I had just come home after playing cricket on the maidan. I had taken my meal and now I was rummaging in a box of old books and family heirlooms that had just that day been brought out of the attic by my grandmother. Nothing in the box interested me very much except for a book with colourful pictures of birds and butterflies. I was going through the book, looking at the pictures, when I found a small photograph between the pages. It was a faded picture, a little yellow and foggy. It was the picture of a girl standing against a wall and behind the wall there was nothing but sky. But from the other side a pair of hands reached up, as though someone was going to climb the wall. There were flowers growing near the girl but I couldn't tell what they were. There was a creeper too but it was just a creeper.

I ran out into the garden. 'Granny!' I shouted. 'Look at this picture! I found it in the box of old things. Whose picture is it?'

I jumped on the bed beside my grandmother and she walloped me on the bottom and said, 'Now I've lost count of my stitches and the next time you do that I'll make you finish the scarf yourself.'

Granny was always threatening to teach me how to knit which I thought was a disgraceful thing for a boy to do. It was a good deterrent for keeping me out of mischief. Once I had torn the drawing room curtains and Granny had put a needle and thread in my hand and made me stitch the curtain together, even though I could only make long, two-inch stitches, which had to be taken out by Grandmother and done again.

She now took the photograph from my hand and

we both stared at it for quite a long time. The girl had long, loose hair and she wore a long dress that nearly covered her ankles, and sleeves that reached her wrists, and there were a lot of bangles on her hands. But despite all this drapery, the girl appeared to be full of freedom and movement. She stood with her legs apart and her hands on her hips and had a wide, almost devilish smile on her face.

'Whose picture is it?' I asked.

'A little girl's, of course,' said Grandmother. 'Can't you tell?'

'Yes, but did you know the girl?'

'Yes. I knew her,' said Granny, 'but she was a very wicked girl and I shouldn't tell you about her. But I'll tell you about the photograph. It was taken about sixty years ago in front of the garden wall.'

'Whose hands are they,' I asked, 'coming up from the other side?'

Grandmother squinted and looked closely at the picture, and shook her head. 'It's the first time I've noticed,' she said. 'They must have been the sweeper boy's. Or maybe they were your grandfather's.'

'They don't look like Grandfather's hands,' I said. 'His hands were all bony.'

'Yes, but this was sixty years ago.'

'Didn't he climb up the wall after the photo?'

'No, nobody climbed up. At least, I don't remember.'

'And you remember well, Granny.'

'Yes, I remember . . . I remember what is not in the photograph. It was a spring day and there was a cool breeze blowing, nothing like this. Those flowers at the girl's feet, they were marigolds, and the bougainvillaea creeper, it was a mass of purple. You cannot see these colours in the photo and even if you could, as nowadays, you wouldn't be able to smell the flowers or feel the breeze.'

'And what about the girl?' I said. 'Tell me about the girl.'

'Well, she was a wicked girl,' said Granny. 'You don't know the trouble they had getting her into those fine clothes she's wearing.'

'I think they are terrible clothes,' I said.

'So did she. Most of the time, she hardly wore a thing. She used to go swimming in a muddy pool with a lot of ruffianly boys, and ride on the backs of buffaloes. No boy ever teased her, though, because she could kick and scratch and pull his hair out!'

'She looks like it too,' I said. 'You can tell by the way she's smiling. At any moment something's going to happen.'

'Something did happen,' said Granny. 'Her mother wouldn't let her take off the clothes afterwards, so she went swimming in them, and lay for half an hour in the mud.'

I laughed heartily and Grandmother laughed too.

'Who was the girl?' I said. 'You must tell me who she was.'

'No, that wouldn't do,' said Grandmother, but I pretended I didn't know. I knew, because Grandmother still smiled in the same way, even though she didn't have as many teeth.

'Come on, Granny,' I said, 'tell me, tell me.'

But Grandmother shook her head and carried on with the knitting. And I held the photograph in my hand looking from it to my grandmother and back again, trying to find points in common between the old lady and the little pig-tailed girl. A lemon-coloured butterfly settled on the end of Grandmother's knitting needle and stayed there while the needles clicked away. I made a grab at the butterfly and it flew off in a dipping flight and settled on a sunflower.

'I wonder whose hands they were,' whispered Grandmother to herself, with her head bowed, and her needles clicking away in the soft warm silence of that summer afternoon.

The Funeral

'I DON'T THINK he should go,' said Aunt Mabel.

'He's too small,' concurred Aunt Beryl. 'He'll get upset, and probably throw a tantrum. And you know Padre Lal doesn't like having children at funerals.'

They were talking about me, but I said nothing. I sat in the darkest corner of the darkened room, my face revealing nothing of what I thought and felt. My father's coffin lay in the next room, the lid fastened forever over the tired, wistful countenance of the man who had meant so much to me. Nobody else had really mattered— neither uncles nor aunts nor fond grandparents. Least of all my mother who had been hundreds of miles away with another husband all these years.

I hadn't seen her since I was four—that was just over seven years ago. I had very dim memories of her. Most other children had their mothers with them, and I found it a bit strange that mine couldn't stay.

Whenever I asked my father *why* she'd gone, he'd say, 'You'll understand when you grow up.' And if I asked him *where* she'd gone, he'd look troubled and say, 'I really don't know.' This was the only question of mine to which he didn't have an answer.

I had not been able to recognize my mother today— she had dropped in with her husband earlier in the day to express her condolences to Granny and to comfort me. Apparently they were moving into a house in Dehra soon enough. They asked me about boarding school. Later I heard them telling Granny, Uncle Ken, Aunt Beryl and Aunt Mabel that it was only proper for me to stay with them after my annual school examinations. After all, how could Granny be expected to take care of a growing boy like me? Though my feelings in this matter were not taken into account I wanted to tell them that I wanted no one at all, except perhaps Granny. But somehow I felt too detached to say anything at all in the end.

Grandma's house was full of people—friends, relatives, neighbours. Some had tried to fuss over me but had been discouraged by my silence, the absence of tears. The more understanding of them had kept their distance. Granny was too devastated herself to offer any solace to me.

Scattered words of condolence passed back and forth

like dragonflies on the wind. 'Such a tragedy!' . . . 'Only forty-one' . . . 'No one realized how serious it was' . . . 'Devoted to the child' . . .

It seemed to me that everyone who mattered in the hill station of Dehra was present. This was ironical for my father had not been a sociable man. Books, music, flowers and his stamp collection had been his main preoccupations, apart from me. Also, he had been away from Dehra for quite sometime now because his job required him to travel a lot.

A small hearse, drawn by a hill pony, was led in at the gate and several able-bodied men lifted the coffin and manoeuvred it into the carriage. The crowd drifted away. The cemetery was about a mile down the road and those who did not have cars would have to walk the distance.

I stared through a window at the small procession passing through the gate. I'd been forgotten for the moment—left in care of Ayah and Puran. Granny had been forbidden from attending Father's funeral because everyone thought she was too frail and stunned to withstand the ordeal. She had retired to her room in painful silence. Outside, it was misty. The mist had crept up the valley and settled like a damp towel on the face of the mountain. Everyone was wet although it hadn't rained.

I waited until everyone had gone and then I left the room and went out on the veranda. Puran, who had been sitting in a bed of nasturtiums, looked up and asked me if I needed anything. But I shook my head and retreated indoors. The gardener, looking aggrieved because of the damage done to the flower beds by the mourners, shambled off to his quarters. The sahib's death could very well mean that he would be out of a job very soon. The house might pass into other hands if the sahib's mother decided to leave for England with the boy. There weren't many people who kept gardeners these days. In the kitchen, Ayah was busy preparing the only big meal ever served in the house. All those relatives, and the Padre too, would come back famished, ready for a sombre but nevertheless substantial meal.

I slipped out of the house by a back door and made my way into the lane through a gap in a thicket of dog roses. When I reached the main road, I could see the mourners wending their way round the hill to the cemetery. I followed at a distance.

It was the same road I had often taken with Father during our evening walks. I knew the name of almost every plant and wildflower that grew on the hillside. These, and various birds and insects, had been described and pointed out to me by my father.

Looking northwards, I could see the higher ranges

of the Himalayas and the eternal snows. The graves in the cemetery were so laid out that if their incumbents did happen to rise one day, the first thing they would see would be the glint of the sun on those snow-covered peaks. Possibly the site had been chosen for the view. But to me it did not seem as if anyone would be able to thrust aside those massive tombstones and rise from their graves to enjoy the view. Their rest seemed as eternal as the snows. It would take an earthquake to burst those stones asunder and thrust the coffins up from the earth. I wondered why people hadn't made it easier for the dead to rise. They were so securely entombed that it appeared as though no one really wanted them to get out.

'God has need of your father . . .' With those words a well-meaning missionary had tried to console me.

And had God, in the same way, laid claim to the thousands of men, women and children who had been put to rest here in these neat and serried rows? What could He have wanted them for? Of what use are we to God when we are dead, I wondered.

The cemetery gate stood open but I leant against the old stone wall and stared down at the mourners as they shuffled about with the unease of a batsman about to face a very fast bowler. Only this bowler was invisible and would come up stealthily and from behind.

Padre Lal's voice droned on through the funeral service and then the coffin was lowered—down, deep down—I was surprised at how far down it seemed to go! Was that other, better world down in the depths of the earth? How could anyone, even a Samson, push his way back to the surface again? Superman did it in comics but my father was a gentle soul who wouldn't fight too hard against the earth and the grass and the roots of tiny trees. Or perhaps he'd grow into a tree and escape that way! 'If ever I'm put away like this,' I thought, 'I'll get into the root of a plant and then I'll become a flower and then maybe a bird will come and carry my seed away . . . I'll get out somehow!'

A few more words from the Padre and then some of those present threw handfuls of earth over the coffin before moving away.

Slowly, in twos and threes, the mourners departed. The mist swallowed them up. They did not see me standing behind the wall. They were getting hungry.

I stood there until they had all gone. Then I noticed that the gardeners or caretakers were filling in the grave. I did not know whether to go forward or not. I was a little afraid. And it was too late now. The grave was almost covered.

I turned and walked away from the cemetery. The road stretched ahead of me, empty, swathed in mist.

I was alone. What had Father said to me once? 'The strongest man in the world is he who stands alone.'

Well, I was alone (Granny and my uncles and aunts did not really count), but at the moment I did not feel very strong.

For a moment I thought my father was beside me, that we were together on one of our long walks. Instinctively, I put out my hand, expecting my father's warm, comforting touch. But there was nothing there, nothing, no one . . .

I clenched my fists and pushed them deep down into my pockets. I lowered my head so that no one would see my tears. There were people in the mist but I did not want to go near them for they had put my father away.

'He'll find a way out,' I said fiercely to myself. 'He'll get out somehow!'

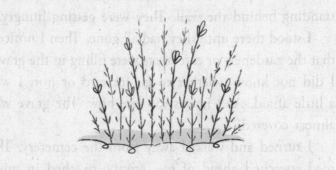

Coming Home to Dehra

THE FAINT QUEASINESS I always feel towards the end of a journey probably has its origin in that first homecoming after my father's death.

It was the winter of 1942—yes, a long time ago—and the train was running through the thick sal forests near Dehra, bringing me at every click of the rails nearer to the mother I hadn't seen for seven years and the stepfather I had seen just once or twice before my parents were divorced.

I was eleven and I was coming home to my mother and stepfather in Dehra.

It was only last summer that I had gone to spend my school holidays with my father. We were very happy together. He was serving in the RAF, at New Delhi, and we lived in a large tent somewhere near Humayun's tomb. The area is now a very busy part of urban Delhi, but in those days it was still a wilderness of scrub jungle where black buck and nilgai roamed freely. We took long walks together, exploring the ruins of old tombs and forts; went to the pictures (George Formby comedies were special favourites of mine); collected stamps; bought books; and made plans for going to England with Granny when the war was over.

Two months of bliss, even though it was summer and there weren't any fans, only a thick khus reed curtain which had to be splashed with water every hour by a *bhisti* (water-carrier) who did the rounds of similar tents with his goatskin water bag. I remember the tender refreshing fragrance of the khus, and also the smell of damp earth outside, where the water had spilt.

A happy time. But it had to end even before my summer vacation was over. My father's periodic bouts of malarial fever resulted in his having to enter hospital for a week. The *bhisti*'s small son came to stay with me at night, and during the day I took my meals with an Anglo-Indian family across the road.

I would have been quite happy to continue with this arrangement, but someone at Air Headquarters must have advised Father to send me back to boarding school. Reluctantly, he came to the decision that this would be the best thing and we parted unhappily.

This is not the story of my life at boarding school. It might easily have been a public school in England;

it did in fact pride itself on being the 'Eton of the East'. The traditions—such as ragging and flogging, compulsory games and chapel attendance, prefects larger than life, and Honour Boards for everything from school captaincy to choir membership—had all apparently been borrowed from *Tom Brown's Schooldays*.

My father wrote to me regularly as soon as he got well, and his letters were the things I looked forward to more than anything else. He came to Simla during my midterm break and took me out for the duration of the holidays. We stayed in a hotel called Craig-Dhu, on a spur north of Jacko Hill. It was an idyllic week—long walks; stories about phantom rickshaws; ice creams in the sun; browsings in bookshops; more plans ('We will go to England next year.').

School seemed a stupid and heartless place after my father had gone away. He had been transferred to Calcutta and he wasn't keeping well there. Malaria again. And then jaundice. But his last letter sounded quite cheerful. He'd been selling part of his valuable stamp collection so as to have enough money for the fares to England.

One day my classteacher sent for me.

'I want to talk to you, Bond,' he said. 'Let's go for a walk.'

I knew immediately that something was wrong.

We took the path that went through the deodar forest, past Council Rock where Scout meetings were held. As soon as my unfortunate teacher (no doubt cursing the Headmaster for having given him this unpleasant task) started on the theme of 'God wanting your father in a higher and better place' as though there could be any better place than Jacko Hill in midsummer, I knew my father was dead, and burst into tears.

They let me stay in the school hospital for a few days until I felt better. The Headmaster visited me there and took away the pile of my father's letters that I'd kept beside me.

'Your father's letters. You might lose them. Why not leave them with me? Then at the end of the year, before you go home, you can come and collect them.'

Unwillingly, I gave him the letters. He told me he'd heard from my mother that I would be going home to her at the end of the year. He seemed surprised that I evinced no interest in this prospect.

At the end of the year, the day before school closed, I went to the HM's office and asked for my letters.

'What letters?' he said. His desk was piled with papers and correspondence, and he was irritated by my interruption.

'My father's letters,' I explained. 'I gave them to you to keep for me, Sir—when he died . . .'

'Letters. Are you sure you gave them to me?'

He grew more irritated. 'You must be mistaken, Bond. Why should *I* want to keep *your* father's letters?'

'I don't know, Sir. You said I could collect them before going home.'

'Look, I don't remember any letters and I'm very busy just now, so run along. I'm sure you're mistaken, but if I find your letters, I'll send them to you.'

I don't suppose he meant to be unkind, but he was the first man who aroused in me feelings of hate . . .

As the train drew into Dehra, I looked out of the window to see if there was anyone on the platform waiting to receive me. The station was crowded enough, as most railway stations are in India, with overloaded travellers, shouting coolies, stray dogs, stray stationmasters . . . Pandemonium broke loose as the train came to a halt and people debauched from the carriages. I was thrust on the platform with my tin trunk and small attaché case. I sat on the trunk and waited for someone to find me.

Slowly, the crowd melted away. I was left with one elderly coolie who was too feeble to carry heavy luggage and had decided that my trunk was just the right size and weight for his head and shoulders. I waited another

ten minutes, but no representative of my mother or stepfather appeared. I permitted the coolie to lead me out of the station to the tonga stand.

Those were the days when everyone, including high-ranking officials, went about in tongas. I was quite happy sitting beside a rather smelly, paan-spitting tonga-driver, while his weary, underfed pony clip-clopped along the quiet tree-lined roads.

The roads were lined with neem and mango trees, eucalyptus, Persian lilac, jacaranda, amaltas (laburnum) and many others. In the gardens of the bungalows were mangoes, litchis and guavas; sometimes jackfruit and papaya. For once, though, I was not stirred by the sight of all these trees; I was too preoccupied with unnamed thoughts and fears about sharing my life with Mother and stepfather— virtual strangers to me.

The tonga first took me to my grandmother's house. I was under the impression that my mother might be waiting for me there.

My grandmother's lovely, comfortable bungalow spread itself about the grounds in an easy-going old-fashioned way. The smoke coming from the chimneys reminded me of the smoke from my grandfather's pipe. But Grandfather was dead. And so was Father. Grandmother now lived alone.

White-haired, but still broad in the face and even broader behind, she was astonished to see me getting down from the tonga.

'Didn't anyone meet you at the station?' she asked.

I shook my head. Grandmother said: 'Your mother hasn't visited me for quite some time now. You can come in and wait, but she may be worried about you, so I'd better take you to her place. Come on, help me up into the tonga . . . I might have known it would be a white horse. It always makes me nervous sitting in a tonga behind a white horse.'

'Why Granny?'

'I don't know, I suppose white horses are nervous too. Anyway, they are always trying to topple me out. Not so fast, driver!' she called out, as the tonga-man cracked his whip and the pony changed from a slow shuffle to a brisk trot.

It took us about twenty-five minutes to reach my stepfather's house which was in the Dalanwala area, not far from the dry bed of the seasonal Rispana river. My grandmother, seeing that I was in need of moral support, got down with me, while the tonga-driver carried my bedding-roll and tin trunk on to the veranda. The front door was bolted from inside. We had to knock on it repeatedly and call out before it was opened by a servant who did not look pleased at being disturbed. When he saw my grandmother, he gave her a deferential salaam, then gazed at me with open curiosity.

'Where's the memsahib?' asked Grandmother.

'Out,' said the servant.

'I can see that, but where have they gone?'

'They went yesterday to Motichur, for shikar. They will be back this evening.'

Grandmother looked upset, but motioned to the servant to bring in my things. 'Weren't they expecting the boy?' she asked.

'Yes,' he said looking at me again. 'But they said he would be arriving tomorrow.'

'They've forgotten the date,' said Grandmother in a huff. 'Anyway, you can unpack and have a wash and change your clothes.'

Turning to the servant, she asked, 'Is there any lunch?'

'I will make lunch,' he said. He was staring at me again, and I felt uneasy with his eyes on me. He was tall and swarthy, with oily, jet-black hair and a thick moustache. A heavy scar ran down his left cheek, giving him a rather sinister appearance. He wore a torn shirt and dirty pyjamas. His broad, heavy feet were wet. They left marks on the uncarpeted floor.

A baby was crying in the next room, and presently a

woman (who turned out to be the cook's wife) appeared in the doorway, jogging the child in her arms.

'They've left the baby behind, too,' said Grandmother, becoming more and more irate. 'He is your brother. Only six months old.' I hadn't been told anything about a younger brother. The discovery that I had one came as something of a shock. I wasn't prepared for a baby brother, least of all a baby half-brother. I examined the child without much enthusiasm. He looked healthy enough and he cried with gusto.

'He's a beautiful baby,' said Grandmother. 'Well I've got work to do. The servants will look after you. You can come and see me in a day or two. You've grown since I last saw you. And you're getting pimples.'

This reference to my appearance did not displease me as Grandmother never indulged in praise. For her to have observed my pimples indicated that she was fond of me.

The tonga-driver was waiting for her. 'I suppose I'll have to use the same tonga,' she said. 'Whenever I need a tonga, they disappear, except for the ones with white ponies . . . When your mother gets back, tell her I want to see her. Shikar, indeed. An infant to look after, and they've gone shooting.'

Grandmother settled herself in the tonga, nodded in response to the cook's salaam, and took a tight grip of the armrests of her seat. The driver flourished his whip and the pony set off at the same listless, unhurried trot, while my grandmother, feeling quite certain that she was going to be hurtled to her doom by a wild white pony, set her teeth and clung tenaciously to the tonga seat. I was sorry to see her go.

My mother and stepfather returned in the evening from their hunting trip with a pheasant which was duly handed over to the cook, whose name was Mangal Singh. My mother gave me a perfunctory kiss. I think she was pleased to see me, but I was accustomed to a more intimate caress from my father, and the strange reception I had received made me realize the extent of my loss. Boarding school life had been routine. Going home was something that I had always looked forward to. But going home had usually meant going to my father—unless I went to Granny's place. But now Father had vanished and I was left quite desolate.

I had heard that if one is present when a loved one dies, or sees him dead and laid out and later buried, one is convinced of the finality of the thing and finds it easier to adapt to the changed circumstances. Though my father's funeral was tangible evidence of his death, I felt as if he had not actually died, but simply vanished from my life. And although this enabled me to remember him as a living, smiling, breathing person, it meant that I was not wholly reconciled to his death, and subconsciously expected him to turn up (as he often did, when I most needed him) and deliver me from an unpleasant situation.

My stepfather barely noticed me. The first thing he did on coming into the house was to pour himself a whisky and soda. My mother, after inspecting the baby, did likewise. I was left to unpack and settle in my room.

I was fortunate in having my own room. I was as desirous of my own privacy as my mother and stepfather were desirous of theirs. My stepfather, a local businessman, was ready to put up with me provided I did not get in the way. And, in a different way, I was ready to put up with him, provided he left me alone. I was even willing that my mother should leave me alone.

There was a big window to my room, and I opened it to the evening breeze, and gazed out on to the garden, a rather unkempt place where marigolds and a sort of wild blue everlasting grew rampant among the litchi trees.

I spent a few restless months with my mother and stepfather till it became evident to all of us that this arrangement wouldn't quite work out. My mother felt she couldn't cope with both—my baby brother and me—all of a sudden, specially when she hadn't bothered about me till now. She wasn't the only one to blame—I felt that I was staying with her merely out of deference for that wish which she had expressed during Father's funeral. I was itching to be back with Granny, and visited her often—much to my stepfather's annoyance and my mother's pique.

Then just as suddenly as they came to Dehra, my mother and stepfather decided to move out. Why such a decision was taken I never really found out—perhaps my stepfather's business wasn't doing well, or they had grown tired of Dehra already. In any case, I could see that they were not too happy about having me on their hands now. Granny, with her uncanny perception, must have sensed this. She expressed her unwillingness to let go of me as I was her only grandchild, and the sole reminder of her son. She said that it would be in the best interests of everyone concerned (especially me) for me to stay back with her and grow up where my father too had spent a considerable part of his life. This relieved my mother and stepfather certainly, but it was I who was most moved and excited by Granny's kind proposal. Finally, I'd be going back to my grandparents' house for good—I was truly going to be back 'at home' in Dehra.

The Wish

LIFE SELDOM TURNS out the way we expect it to. The house in Dehra had to be sold. My father had not left any money; he had never realized that his health would deteriorate so rapidly from the malarial fevers which had grown in frequency. He was still planning for the future when he died. Now that my father was gone, Grandmother saw no point in staying on in India; there was nothing left in the bank and she needed money for our passages to England, so the house had to go. Dr Ghose, who had a thriving medical practice in Dehra, made her a reasonable offer, which she accepted.

Then things happened very quickly. Grandmother sold most of our belongings, because as she said, we wouldn't be able to cope with a lot of luggage. The *kabaris* came in droves, buying up crockery, furniture, carpets and clocks at throwaway prices. Grandmother hated parting with some of her possessions such as the carved giltwood mirror, her walnut-wood armchair and her rosewood writing desk, but it was impossible to take them with us. They were carried away in a bullock cart.

Ayah was very unhappy at first but cheered up when Grandmother got her a job with a tea planter's family in Assam. It was arranged that she could stay with us until we left Dehra.

We went at the end of September, just as the monsoon clouds broke up, scattered and were driven away by soft breezes from the Himalayas. There was no time to revisit the island where my grandfather and I had planted our trees. And in the urgency and excitement of the preparations for our departure, I forgot to recover my small treasures from the hole in the banyan tree. It was only when we were in Bansi's tonga, on the way to the station, that I remembered my top, catapult and Iron Cross. Too late! To go back for them would mean missing the train.

'Hurry!' urged Grandmother nervously. 'We mustn't be late for the train, Bansi.'

Bansi flicked the reins and shouted to his pony, and for once in her life Grandmother submitted to being carried along the road at a brisk trot.

'It's five to nine,' she said, 'and the train leaves at nine.'

'Do not worry, memsahib. I have been taking you to the station for fifteen years, and you have never missed a train!'

'No,' said Grandmother. 'And I don't suppose you'll ever take me to the station again, Bansi.'

'Times are changing, memsahib. Do you know that there is now a taxi—a *motor car*—competing with the tongas of Dehra? You are lucky to be leaving. If you stay, you will see me starve to death!'

'We will all starve to death if we don't catch that train,' said Grandmother.

'Do not worry about the train, it never leaves on time, and no one expects it to. If it left at nine o'clock, everyone would miss it.'

Bansi was right. We arrived at the station at five minutes past nine, and rushed on to the platform, only to find that the train had not yet arrived.

The platform was crowded with people waiting to catch the same train or to meet people arriving on it. Ayah was there already, standing guard over a pile of miscellaneous luggage. We sat down on our boxes and became part of the platform life at an Indian railway station.

Moving among piles of bedding and luggage were sweating, cursing coolies; vendors of magazines, sweetmeats, tea and betel-leaf preparations; also stray dogs, stray people and sometimes a stray stationmaster.

The cries of the vendors mixed with the general clamour of the station and the shunting of a steam engine in the yards. 'Tea, hot tea!' Sweets, papads, hot stuff, cold drinks, tooth powder pictures of film stars, bananas, balloons, wooden toys, clay images of the gods. The platform had become a bazaar.

Ayah was giving me all sorts of warnings.

'Remember, baba, don't lean out of the window when the train is moving. There was that American boy who lost his head last year! And don't eat rubbish at every station between here and Bombay. And see that no strangers enter the compartment. Mr Wilkins was robbed and murdered last year!'

The station bell clanged, and in the distance there appeared a big, puffing steam engine, painted green and gold and black. A stray dog with a lifetime's experience of trains, darted away across the railway lines. As the train came alongside the platform, doors opened, window shutters fell, faces appeared in the openings, and even before the train had come to a stop, people were trying to get in or out.

For a few moments there was chaos. The crowd surged backward and forward. No one could get out. No one could get in. A hundred people were leaving the train, two hundred were getting into it. No one wanted to give way.

The problem was solved by a man climbing out of a window. Others followed his example and the pressure at the doors eased and people started squeezing into their compartments.

Grandmother had taken the precaution of reserving berths in a first-class compartment, and assisted by Bansi and half a dozen coolies, we were soon inside with all our luggage. A whistle blasted and we were off! Bansi had to jump from the running train.

As the engine gathered speed, I ignored Ayah's advice and put my head out of the window to look back at the receding platform. Ayah and Bansi were standing on the platform waving to me, and I kept waving to them until the train rushed into the darkness and the bright lights of Dehra were swallowed up in the night. New lights, dim and flickering, came into existence as we passed small villages. The stars too were visible and I saw a shooting star streaking through the heavens.

I remembered something that Ayah had once told me, that stars are the spirits of good men, and I wondered if that shooting star was a sign from my father that he was aware of our departure and would be with us on our journey. And I remembered something else that Ayah had said—that if one wished on a shooting star, one's wish would be granted, provided, of course, that one thrust all five fingers into the mouth at the same time!

'What on earth are you doing?' asked Grandmother staring at me as I thrust my fist into my mouth.

'Making a wish,' I said.

'Oh,' said Grandmother.

She was preoccupied, and didn't ask me what I was wishing for, nor did I tell her.

We never made it to England. Grandmother passed away after a brief illness in Lucknow. Aunt Emily—in whose house we were staying before going on to Bombay to board our ship to England—made arrangements for her funeral and for me to be sent back to Dehra. My father's cousin Mr John Harrison who lived in Dehra agreed to let me stay with him and attend the day school in the town.

By a strange twist of fate therefore, my wish to return to Dehra was coming true after all. I did not know if it was something to now look forward to, or dread.

Read More in Puffin

Thick as Thieves: Tales of Friendship
Ruskin Bond

Somewhere in life
There must be someone
To take your hand
And share the torrid day.
Without the touch of friendship
There is no life and we must fade away.

Discover a hidden pool with three young boys, laugh out loud as a little mouse makes demands on a lonely writer, follow the mischievous 'four feathers' as they discover a baby lost in the hills and witness the bond between a tiger and his master. Some stories will make you smile, some will bring tears to your eyes, some may make your heart skip a beat but all of them will renew your faith in the power of friendship.

Read More in Puffin

Uncles, Aunts and Elephants:
Tales from your Favourite Storyteller
Ruskin Bond

I know the world's a crowded place,
And elephants do take up space,
But if it makes a difference, Lord,
I'd gladly share my room and board.
A baby elephant would do...
But, if he brings his mother too,
There's Dad's garage. He wouldn't mind.
To elephants, he's more than kind.
But I wonder what my Mum would say
If their aunts and uncles came to stay!

Ruskin Bond has entertained generations of readers for many decades. This delightful collection of poetry, prose and non-fiction brings together some of his best work in a single volume. Sumptuously illustrated, *Uncles, Aunts and Elephants* is a book to treasure for all times.